MIDNIGHT KISSES

ALEXA RIVERS

To Shannon
For always being in my corner.

1

ake that, Chloe Somers.

Emily Parker shook her fall of long red hair out of the way and scrutinized the bridal bouquet—an arrangement of white orchids and roses. Satisfied, she placed it in the center of the wedding party's table. She tweaked a single flower that had drooped, and adjusted the ribbon holding the bouquet together. *Perfect.* No one could possibly accuse her of doing a sub-par job just because she loathed the bride, not when she'd pulled together a masterpiece with hardly any notice. Moving on from the bridal bouquet, she set out four smaller bouquets in front of the seats marked for the bridesmaids and grooms-men. She eyed them critically.

Everything had to be just right.

Even though she would prefer not to be involved with this wedding—the second Chloe Somers wedding she'd been hired to decorate—she couldn't afford to turn down work. Not in a town the size of Attiring, despite it becoming something of a wedding destination. Another year or two and she had no doubt her floristry business would be booming just like her gift store and commercial rental business. Happy couples were drawn to Itirangi by the gorgeous backdrop—the azure lake that was glacier-fed and the stunning green-brown of the surrounding mountains and forests. The picture-perfect New Zealand town.

Over the past few weeks, foreigners and out-of-towners had descended upon the town in droves for their summer vacations, so Emily's gift shop was bustling, and all of her tenants in the refurbished heritage building she owned—ranging from book stores to artist studios to beauty parlors—were experiencing the same wave of activity. She could barely afford the time away to decorate the vineyard restaurant for Chloe's wedding.

At the thought of Chloe's previous wedding, Emily's stomach lurched uncomfortably. Planned for a little less than a year ago, that first wedding had been canceled two weeks before the big day, when Chloe had dumped the groom to run off with his second cousin—who, incidentally, was the groom of *this* wedding. Emily wanted to drag both Chloe and her fiancé over a field of hot coals.

But that didn't matter. What mattered was that this wedding actually *happen*. Though Emily would be paid either way, she could think of no better punishment for the groom, Rich Belvedere, who'd stolen another man's woman, than to live the rest of his days with Satan's Mistress as his wife. Furthermore, Emily was a professional, and firmly believed that everyone should have a beautiful wedding. She could put her feelings aside for as long as it took to give Chloe her dream wedding, and cash the paycheck.

Strolling outside to her car, Emily took a moment to enjoy the chirping of birds in the trees that ringed the graveled parking lot. The warm wind rustled through the vineyard behind her, carrying with it the scent of leaves and fruit. Sweat beaded on her forehead and she wiped it with the back of a hand. From her car, she retrieved an awkwardly-sized box where she'd stored the table centerpieces and maneuvered it back inside the restaurant, the weight causing her no problems because her arms were toned, accustomed to the heavy lifting.

Hands on hips, she surveyed the reception room, taking stock of the raw materials. A number of long rectangular tables covered by white tablecloths dominated the space, contrasting pleasantly with the wooden walls and floors. The large windows provided a beautiful view out over the vineyard. The place had good bones.

She started assembling the table decorations, an elegant arrangement consisting of silver candlesticks with towering white candles and simple but elegant bouquets. The candlesticks were heavy. She couldn't help but think she wouldn't mind whacking the bride upside her head with one. Gently, of course. Just enough to give her a shock. Payback for running out on a good man, and for the years of torment Emily had endured at her hands in high school.

Carrot top, Chloe had called her. *Chubby cheeks. Ginny Weasley.*

Actually, Emily hadn't minded the last one. But regardless, after being bullied by the gorgeous Queen Bee, she could barely stand to be employed by her. The past few days, Emily had needed every ounce of her patience, and regular sessions watching kitten videos on YouTube, to make it through.

"Hey, Em."

Emily swung around, her smile wavering at the sight of Justin Simons. His broad frame filled the doorway, and his thumbs were hooked into the pockets of his jeans. He looked crazy-handsome despite the faded clothes, the halo of unruly dark hair, and the scruffy beard that hid the lower half of his face. Her silly heart danced a tango in her chest. Justin could crawl guerrilla-style into her house after spending a month battling through the wild forest that bordered Lake Itirangi, and Emily would still think he was the most striking man she'd ever laid eyes on. Hands down.

If childhood bullying was the first reason Emily hated Chloe Somers, then Justin Simons was the second.

"Justin," she said, her voice breathy. "What are you doing here?"

Did he know what today was?

Almost a year ago, Chloe had left him with the responsibility of cancelling their wedding while she skipped town with Rich. It couldn't be a coincidence that he was here now. Did he plan to sabotage the wedding? Try to win Chloe back? The town had been abuzz with speculation after Chloe ended their relationship so spectacularly, and Justin had retreated into his house by the forest, grown a beard, and barely spared a kind word for anyone since. His surliness didn't stop Emily's foolish heart from wishing he'd see her as something other than a little girl, or a friend of his sister.

"Scoping out the wedding," he replied gruffly, shifting from one foot to the other, as if he regretted saying hello and was itching to leave.

She shouldn't be offended. Justin seemed uncomfortable in *anyone's* presence these days. He was more of a loner, spending time with his family but few others. All of the locals desperately wanted to support him, but he wouldn't give them the chance.

"Why?" she asked, wondering if she'd been right about his plan to interfere.

He shrugged one massive shoulder. "I'm invited."

Like he'd pulled the pin on her emotional grenade, Emily exploded. "Oh, for fudge sake! Shiitake mushrooms on a stick with a side of flaming brownies. Are you kidding me right now?"

IF ANYONE else had uttered the ridiculous expletives that had just passed between Emily Parker's pouty pink lips, Justin would have laughed in their face. But Emily looked so adorably angry on his behalf, her entire face flushed red and her tiny fists clenched, body shaking with rage, that he was oddly flattered. Everyone knew Emily was the nicest person in Itirangi, and for her to be furious like this? It meant something. She seemed ready to go to war for him. And Justin, dirty sonofabitch that he was, badly wanted to bend her over one of the dining tables and show her how much he appreciated her support.

Instead, he reigned in the impulse to defile Itirangi's favorite sweetheart and said, "I wouldn't joke about something like that."

"Please say you're not actually coming."

He wished he could. He'd rather be anywhere else. But Chloe and Rich had invited him to their super-romantic New Year's Eve wedding—even if they'd excluded the rest of his family, likely at Chloe's behest—and his pride wouldn't let him reject the invitation. He couldn't bear for them to assume he was pining for Chloe. He wasn't. He was well rid of her. End of story.

So here he was, getting the lay of the land, ready to venture into enemy territory come nightfall. Chloe and Rich had planned the wedding to culminate in a countdown to midnight, complete with fireworks at the moment the year changed. Very romantic, he was sure, for the bride and groom and anyone who had a date, but Justin didn't. He'd RSVP'd with a plus-one, but never got around to finding someone to accompany him. He needed someone trustworthy, but in Itirangi, very few people could be relied on not to gossip. Now that the day was here, he would happily go back in time and kick his own ass for not organizing some kind of moral support.

"I'm coming," he told her, deadly serious.

Emily folded her arms over her breasts, drawing his attention to the curves hidden by a high-necked shirt. He'd fantasized about running his hands over those curves dozens of times in the past few months. Ever since he'd recovered from Chloe's betrayal, Emily had become his obsession. Unfortunately, with her sweet nature and luscious body, Justin wasn't alone in desiring her. Every unattached male in Itirangi between the ages of fifteen and fifty adored her, and Emily was unfailingly friendly to all of them. Of course, she treated kicked puppies the same way. Justin hoped he was more to her than just another kicked puppy.

"But why?" she asked. "Why torture yourself like that? And why on earth would they invite you in the first place? It's too cruel."

He grunted in agreement. "That's what any normal person would think."

But not Chloe and Rich. He doubted it had occurred to them that inviting him would be anything other than polite. They weren't known for being particularly thoughtful people.

"Do you need a hand?" he asked.

That was why he'd come in, after all. He'd felt guilty hiding out in his car, watching Emily lug boxes of decorations back and forth, a job that would take half as much time if he helped.

"No, no, I'm fine." Her cheeks reddened again. "I don't have much left to do. I'm just putting everything together, adding the final touches."

"So tell me what to do and you can get out of here early." He wasn't backing off. Not when he finally had the opportunity for some alone time with Emily.

"Okay," she relented, and rummaged through one of the boxes for a roll of silver table runners he recognized from his own ill-fated wedding. Apparently, Chloe wasn't above recycling. "Put these down the center of the tables with the centerpieces on top. I'll sort out the candles."

Justin fumbled with the delicate fabric, doing his best to lay the first one neatly, so she wouldn't regret accepting his help. He analyzed the runner. Was it off-center? He adjusted it to the right. Checked again. Better. Shifting to the next table, he repeated the actions.

Once he'd finished with the table runners, Emily slapped a pile of folded napkins into his hands and showed him how to distribute them, along with the menus, which were hand-written in a looping script he struggled to read. He could see signs of Chloe everywhere, and none of her fiancé. But then, perhaps Rich didn't mind someone else being in charge. Unlike Justin, who preferred to make decisions together.

He and Chloe had squabbled like children over just about everything when they were planning to get married: the venue, food, decorations, number of guests invited. Justin had wanted a casual wedding near the forest, while Chloe had wanted something high-end and less outdoorsy. His job as a park ranger had been a constant cause of friction between them. He'd mistakenly imagined they were one of those 'opposites attract' stories, but it turned out that wasn't what she'd wanted at all.

A light touch brushed his flannel-clad upper arm. "You okay?"

He came to with a jolt. Emily's unusual green eyes were watching him with concern. He focused on the darker band around her pupils.

"Fine," he snapped. He wasn't about to fall apart on her, and he'd appreciate it if she didn't look at him like he might. "What now?"

Emily's pulse hammered as she touched Justin. It was the first time she'd been brave enough to initiate contact, but he'd seemed so lost staring at the decorations, as if they held the answers to everything, that she couldn't help it.

She should have made him leave.

Bad enough he was attending the wedding, it must be awful

to help her set it up when the memory of the decor he'd chosen for his wedding was still fresh.

"You go home," she said gently. "I shouldn't have taken advantage of your offer, but thank you for your help."

Justin scowled and brushed her off. "You're not sending me away that easy, Em."

"But—"

"No."

"Tell you what," she said, feeling uncharacteristically bold. "You tell me why you're going to the wedding and I'll let you stay and help me."

She didn't usually ask intrusive questions, but this was Justin, and she finally had him to herself. She'd ask what she wanted to and hopefully make an impression. And part of her really, really wanted to know if he pined after Chloe.

His eyes narrowed, and she thought he might tell her to go to hell, but then he spoke. "I need to save face. If I don't come, all of the old gossips will tear me apart."

"No, they won't!" Emily protested, horrified he'd believe that. Her hand flew to her chest. "Everyone around here loves you, Justin. They only want the best for you."

"But a little fodder for the gossip mill never hurt."

His shoulders were square, his expression stubborn. She could see she wouldn't win this battle, so she passed him a stack of chair covers and demonstrated how to put them in place.

"That easy," she said, tying the bow with a flourish.

Justin's first attempt was such a pitiful mess she couldn't help laughing. Initially indignant, he joined in when she snorted, her eyes widening in horror. She suspected he was laughing more at her snort than his poor efforts, but she went through the motions again, emphasizing each movement as he copied her.

"Like this. Slip it over, shimmy it down. Yes, yes, wait. Hang on a minute." She caught his hand, gnawing on her lower lip as she realized her mistake in touching him again. His callouses rubbed against her fingertips, sending a frisson of awareness up the inside of her arm. His quick intake of breath made her wonder if he'd felt electricity zap between them, too. She studied his hands discreetly, wondering whether the rest of him was equally well built.

Tearing her attention away, she corrected his mistake, and together they tidied up his second chair. He completed the third on his own, and it wasn't bad for a guy with such thick, rough fingers. They finished in under an hour. She cast an eye over his work, making sure it met her rigorous standards—she couldn't have an unhappy customer—then, before she lost her nerve, she hugged him.

Oh, my.

She'd known he was brawny, that much was obvious. Now, being pressed against a wall of muscle, she was inclined to think of him as the Incredible Hulk. All of that body mass made a girl feel delicate. She wanted to explore the bands of muscle with her hands, to learn the way they tensed when he was in the throes of passion.

But no, this was a simple thank you hug. At his ex's wedding venue for crying out loud. She shouldn't be lusting after him.

"Thank you," she said, lurching backward so quickly she narrowly avoided tripping over an empty box. "That would have taken me twice as long without you."

"We're done?"

"Sure are. I'll come back tomorrow to collect my things, but everything is finished for today."

He grunted. Did the man ever use his words?

"Are you certain about going tonight?" she asked, reluctant to let it go. "I can't talk you out of it?"

He nodded decisively. "I'm going. But…"

"But?"

He gazed into the distance for a moment and she wondered whether he'd ignored her, but then he leveled his intense hazel gaze on her. "It might make the time pass faster if you came with me."

Emily's head spun like she'd tripped head over heels into a different dimension. "Excuse me?"

"I understand if it would be too awkward for you," he said, his gaze slipping from hers. "Since you two never got along. But we had fun just now, didn't we?"

"We did," she replied slowly. "But Justin, it's the day of the wedding. You can't just add someone to the guest list."

"Not a problem," he declared. "I said I'd bring a date when I RSVP'd. But—"

"You were too embarrassed to ask anyone," she broke in, understanding immediately.

He shuffled from foot to foot, clearly nervous about her reply. His uncertainty was what undid her.

"Of course I'll come. I'd love to keep you company."

"Thanks." The word was short and sharp, but the gratitude in his eyes warmed her. He might not communicate well verbally, but his body language filled the gaps.

Her foolish heart flip-flopped. This was *Justin.* The prospect of seeing him in a suit had her panting in anticipation.

"I'll pick you up at six," he told her. "The ceremony starts at six thirty, then we'll have dinner. It ends at midnight. Does that suit?"

Emily nodded, worried if she spoke, she wouldn't be able to disguise her sudden eagerness for the evening ahead.

"Bye," she squeaked, as he left.

He lifted a hand in a casual wave.

oly shit.

If Justin had salivated over Emily earlier, it was nothing compared to his reaction when he collected her from her doorstep. His body went into hyperdrive. He was accustomed to her being curvy and cute. But in a deep green dress with a plunging neckline and a slit up the thigh, with chunky black pumps doing amazing things for her legs, he had to tighten his grip on the steering wheel to prevent himself from grabbing her and ripping the dress off.

The woman was built for sin. Her creamy cleavage played peek-a-boo, and he wanted to latch onto the exposed mounds of her breasts with his mouth. He wondered what color her nipples would be. Pale pink or apricot, he guessed, to match her complexion. With effort, he lifted his gaze to her face, only to be captured anew. She'd done something to darken her lashes and bring out the green of her eyes. Her lips glistened bubblegum pink.

"Wow," he said stupidly. "You, um…"

Great work, man. She'll be eating up those sweet words.

To his surprise, she beamed. "Best response a girl can hope for."

Was she humoring him? With most women, he'd assume so, but Emily seemed genuinely pleased.

"You clean up nice," she carried on, apparently unconcerned by his inability to form a coherent sentence. Her green gaze raked over him from head to toe and she nodded approvingly. "Very nice."

"Uh, thanks." *Smooth, Justin. Real smooth.*

For the remainder of the drive to the vineyard, about half an hour, they didn't speak. Normally he didn't worry about participating in small talk for the sake of someone else's comfort, but for once he wished he had the same silver tongue his brother, Cooper, had been blessed with. He longed to fill the silence with witty banter, or to butter her up with compliments until she was ready to strip naked and go at it in the back seat.

Observing her out of the corner of his eye, he noticed how the faint smile she wore never left her lips. He'd always thought Emily's perpetual cheerfulness must be an act, but it seemed he'd been wrong. Either that or being here with him had brought a smile to her face.

Yeah, right.

They passed by golden fields, the grass crisped by the midsummer sun. In the twilight, the heat from the sun had cooled enough to stop the tar on the road from melting, but slicks of black amongst the gray indicated that hadn't been the case all day. He veered around the larger patches. Eventually, the golden fields to his right gave way to rows of grapevines with large green leaves and heavy loads of fruit.

The restaurant came into sight, and he pulled down the driveway and parked beneath the same tree he had earlier. He hurried around to help Emily out. When she took his hand, his gut wrenched with desire at the feel of her smooth, silky skin. Sparks seemed to hum in the air between them as he steadied her with an arm around her waist. Her hair tickled the side of his face and he inhaled the scent of her shampoo, sweet and fruity. Did *everything* about her have to be so appealing?

"Thanks," she murmured, smiling up at him.

He fought the urge to brush a kiss over those glossy lips. "Yeah, no worries. Come on. Let's get inside."

He ushered her into the restaurant and out through the other side, to a roofed pavilion. A steel arch, heavily adorned with white roses and greenery, stood at the end of an aisle edged by posies of pale pink roses and flowing white fabric. He'd wager that Chloe had selected the decorations.

Rich and two of his private school friends, who Justin vaguely recognized, loitered beneath the arch. Rich wore a white tuxedo with a black shirt and a white bow tie. His blond hair was slicked back, and even from a distance, Justin could tell sweat was beading on his hairline and upper lip. *Enjoy the good looks while you can.* The stress of marrying Chloe would age him ten years in no time.

More than half of the seats had already filled—Justin had timed their arrival so they wouldn't have to linger and chat with others. Placing a hand on the small of Emily's back, grateful to have her there as a distraction, he guided her into a seat in the back row. Over the next few minutes, people trickled into the other unoccupied seats. Justin tensed as he caught sight of a married couple that he and Chloe used to be friends with. They'd chosen to stay in touch with Chloe rather than him after the split.

"How many on the guest list?" he asked.

"About two hundred and fifty," Emily replied, keeping her voice low as if to avoid attention.

"Goddamn."

Chloe really had got everything she wanted this time around. Justin had insisted they cull their invite list down to a modest ninety.

"A bit different from what you had planned?"

"You can say that again."

Finally, the bridal procession music started to play. Justin gritted his teeth and mentally prepared to see his ex, up close, for the first time since she'd walked out on him.

~

SHE'S BEAUTIFUL.

No denying it, Chloe Somers was a stunning woman. Her golden-blonde hair was twisted elegantly atop her head, a few tresses spilling down her back. Perfectly made up and attired in a designer wedding gown, she could have been a Hollywood A-lister. In comparison, Emily felt like a frump. If Chloe had aimed to be the most beautiful woman present at her wedding, mission accomplished.

Beside her, Justin fidgeted. Glancing down, Emily noticed his fists were clenched so hard his knuckles had turned white. Poor guy. This had to be hard for him. Prizing one of his hands from his knees, she clasped it in her own. His fingers were cold and clammy. She squeezed, hoping to reassure him. He squeezed back.

The ceremony passed with much fanfare, but Emily didn't hear anything, her attention centered on the man next to her, attuned to his every breath, every move. She heard him scoff once or twice during the vows, but he didn't look away from the bride and groom, not even during the big kiss. She tried not to let the tension emanating from him get to her. She was here for support, which meant she needed to weather any strain with a smile. Now was not the time to let her discomfort with interpersonal issues get the better of her.

When the celebrant pronounced Rich and Chloe husband and wife, indicating the end of the ceremony, friends and family crowded the happy couple, eager to extend their blessings. Emily and Justin stayed put. When the photographer started gathering groups for the family photos, they slipped inside the reception room and found places designated for them at one of the long tables. Dinner was due to begin as soon as family photos were complete. From her involvement in the wedding planning, Emily knew the bridal party photos had already been taken earlier in the day, when the lighting was better.

Emily scanned the other name cards on their table. She recognized a few names. Would Justin? He wasn't as social as she, or exposed to the community as often, but he and Chloe must share a circle of acquaintances to a certain extent.

"Do you know any of these people?"

Justin nodded. "These ones," he pointed to the seats across from theirs, "were mutual friends of Chloe and I when we were together. So were the couples on either side of us."

Awkward. "I guess it must be hard when you'd been together for so long. You grew up knowing the same people."

"Yeah." She couldn't read his expression. "But you quickly learn who your real friends are," he added.

Hopefully he considered her a friend. At the very least, she wanted to be someone he could count on. She murmured agreement. Enough depressing stuff.

"How's your work going at the moment?" she asked. "Must be a busy time of year for you."

"It is," he agreed. "Lots of people on the trails and a lot of maintenance work is needed on the huts and tracks."

"Long days?"

"Yeah, but it's my favorite time of year, so I don't mind." For the first time since they'd arrived this evening, he smiled. Emily cheered internally. "The birds are out singing every day and the sun is shining. Prime work conditions."

Many times over the years, Emily had seen Justin around in his khaki ranger uniform. It made him look virile and capable. Very sexy. Not that he needed any help in that department.

"Sometimes I wish I could spend a little more time out in nature," she confessed. "But working with flowers gives me a taste of it. That's why I won't hire another florist, even though it would allow me more time to manage the gift store and my tenants. Sure, business is interesting, but I love creating pretty things with my hands even more."

"So, that's where it comes from," Justin said.

"What?"

"The name of your shop."

"Ah, right." She'd named her floristry and gift shop 'Pretty Things,' and he was spot on about her reasoning.

"You must put in a lot of hours to stay on top of things."

His upper arm brushed her shoulder and she instinctively leaned into him, expecting him to pull away, but instead he lowered his head until she could feel his breath on the shell of her ear. Goosebumps rippled up her arms.

"I do," she said shakily, "but like you, it's not a hardship, since I love my job."

He laughed, husky and low. "Nice to know we're doing something right, isn't it?"

"We're doing plenty right," she replied firmly. After all, they both had stable jobs they enjoyed, good friends, and nice homes. Things could be much worse. She liked her life. The only thing that might improve it was the man beside her.

Before long, others joined them. Emily focused on remembering names and faces. She made idle small talk, got them laughing. Most seemed to be nice people. Justin barely spoke, seemingly content to let her keep the conversation flowing, which was fine by her. That was her forte at work too. The longer people chatted in her shop, the more they bought, which meant a better bottom line.

THANK GOD FOR EMILY.

She smiled, complimented people, poured drinks from the bottles of wine routinely brought to the table, and generally kept the evening flowing smoothly. Hell, Justin hardly had to say a word; she had him covered. No one needed anything from him with Emily there. He watched her work her magic, admiration blooming deep in his chest. How did she do it? How could she be so ceaselessly nice and unobjectionable that everyone she met liked her?

More than one of his old friends winked at him behind her back or shot him a jealous glance. He puffed with pride. Emily may not technically be his woman, but they didn't know that, and he'd do his level best to earn a chance with her before the night was over. While it was true that she could have any available man in Itirangi with a crook of her finger, the fact she hadn't shown any desire to do so, at least during the year that he'd been paying attention, boded well for him. And yes, she deserved a better man—one who didn't scowl so much and was more even-tempered—but he was too selfish to care.

Before he knew it, dinner had finished. They endured a half-dozen terrible speeches, then the bride and groom took to the dance floor for their first dance. Some forgettable pop song came over the loudspeakers. Another choice of Chloe's, no doubt.

The happy couple swayed together. No one joined them. They wanted the spotlight all to themselves. But when the second song began, Justin claimed Emily's hand and tugged her onto the dance floor. Someone knocked into her back and he took advantage of the jolt to scooch her closer, resting his hand on her hip, no space between their bodies. When she laid her head on his chest and sighed happily, he wondered if she could hear his heart racing.

She did that to him. Drove him crazy.

Slipping his other arm around her, his palm curved into her lower back just above her butt, high enough not to draw attention, but low enough for her to know he had more on his mind than friendship. The curve where her hips flared out begged for his fingers and he longed to explore it more thoroughly.

Emily arched into his embrace, lacing her hands behind his

neck and closing her eyes as she moved in time to the music. The sight of her shuttered eyelids and parted lips illuminated by the soft overhead lighting was so erotic, he had to look away before he embarrassed them both. Thankfully, the next song had a Latin beat, quick and funky, not conducive to slow dancing. A reprieve. Or so he thought, but then Emily's eyes fluttered open and lit with excitement.

Holy hell, he was done for.

Slow dancing with Justin had set fire to Emily's nerve ends. Being pressed against his chiseled chest had aroused her body, while the possessive way he'd held her seduced her heart. She had no answer for it. Then the next song started, and all of the Latin dancing lessons she and her friend Clarissa had taken when they were younger rushed to the front of her mind. She knew this song, and if ever there was a chance to rock Justin's world, this was it.

She tried not to overthink, letting muscle memory take over. She whirled around, the first steps of the salsa coming easily. Justin didn't know the moves, so she improvised, wildly happy when he became slack-jawed with astonishment. And, she hoped, a little lust. Call her crazy, but she thought he might finally see her as a woman.

When the dance petered out, he stopped her and called over the sound of the crowd, "That was hot."

"That was fun!" she exclaimed in response, exhilarated both from the dance and the look in his eye. That dark, heated expression could only be desire. He wanted *her*.

"I'll get us a drink while you catch your breath," he said, leading her from the dance floor then dropping her hand to head to the bar. Emily swayed with the beat as another song started, watching the dancers. Everyone seemed joyful, the way they should at a wedding. The beginning of two people's lifetime together. The most beautiful commitment ever. She smiled.

A man she didn't know appeared in front of her. "Hey, pretty lady. What's your name?"

He grinned, crinkles forming around his vivid blue eyes. His fair hair was cut close to his skull, and while he wasn't much taller than her, his collared shirt clung to his muscular torso and he radiated masculine confidence. She knew his type. Plenty of alpha males had asked her out before. Enough that she could pick one out in a crowd.

Most of the local men didn't push when she said no. They knew she hardly ever dated. She had dated before—she wasn't totally inexperienced—but she rarely found the time or the inclination. She'd been out a handful of times in the past few years but hadn't had a serious boyfriend since her school days, and that had ended when he couldn't envision a future in Itirangi and she couldn't contemplate being anywhere else.

The guy who'd approached her didn't know she'd rather be left alone, and he didn't look as if he would accept a polite dismissal. Her heart sank. Hopefully if she bored him, he'd move on soon enough. She hated confrontation, and some men got ugly when rejected, especially if they weren't aware she turned most people down and took it personally.

"Emily," she replied, not asking for his name in return.

"Em," he confirmed, shortening her name without bothering to ask what she preferred.

Another typical alpha male move, assuming familiarity where there was none. "I'm Sam."

"Nice to meet you." She gazed over his shoulder, trying not to encourage him.

"The pleasure is all mine," he replied with a wink. "Come and dance with me, Em. I saw you out there before and you've got some moves. I'd love to show you mine."

She didn't doubt that. But she'd rather spend her time with a silent hulk who was incapable of doing more than the two-step shuffle. Thankfully, Justin strode back across the room toward them, a glass of champagne in one hand and a beer in the other. When he caught sight of Emily and Sam, he glowered and quickened his pace.

"Hey, baby," he said, ducking to kiss her forehead. He passed her the wine glass and dragged her into an embrace with his newly free arm. "Miss me?" Emily stared at him, dumbstruck. Justin smoldered down at her, then lifted his gaze to Sam, raising an eyebrow in an unspoken challenge. "Introduce me to your new friend."

"Justin, this is Sam," Emily said. The two men engaged in some kind of macho posturing. Emily shrank in on herself, uncomfortable with the tension between them. The men held eye contact until Sam rolled his shoulders, tipped his head to Emily and took off. The moment he was gone, she pulled free of Justin.

"Are men always like that with you?" he asked, apparently concerned.

"You mean, a bit pushy?"

"'A bit' may be an understatement. That guy was pushy as hell."

Emily shrugged one shoulder. "The tourists can be like that. Locals aren't so bad. I should probably be meaner, but you know how I am."

She was too nice for her own good.

"They should see you're uncomfortable and leave you alone," he fired back. He grabbed her shoulders and smoldered again. "Tell me if I'm stepping over a line, but tonight, I want you to be all mine, Emily. And I don't share."

The possessive tone of his voice sent shivers down her spine. "You're not stepping over a line," she whispered, "but what do you want with me, Justin?"

"Right now, I want you all to myself. Walk outside with me?"

She nodded. She could think of nothing she'd rather do.

3

He'd actually done it. Convinced the most beautiful woman at the wedding—bride included—to join him for a romantic stroll in the vineyard. Justin took Emily's hand before she changed her mind and escorted her outside. He decided that even if she was only accompanying him out of gratitude, he'd take it. He had been prepared to brawl on her behalf, and he suspected the guy he'd chased off had known it.

Outside, the light from the moon and a few scattered lamp posts was enough for them to see where they walked but no further, the lamps alternately casting deep shadows over their faces or illuminating them. He tucked Emily's hand into the crook of his arm and savored the brush of her body against his, from knee to shoulders. She'd stirred his blood with those sinuously sensual dance moves, and he desperately wanted to know if she'd move in the same unbelievably sexy way when they were in bed together.

His pants suddenly felt tight. God, he wanted to be inside her. He settled for saying, "I didn't know you could dance like that."

She laughed. "Neither did I. Haven't practiced since high school."

"You're bullshitting me."

She stopped walking and looked up, eyes sincere. "No, really. It's been ages."

"You're telling me you don't whip those moves out when you spot a cute guy at a club?" Even the thought of her twisting around another man made his teeth ache.

"Justin," she murmured. "When would I go to a club? There are none in Itirangi, and as we've already established, I live to work." She shot him a teasing smile. "I spend my spare time doing the books, not meeting cute guys at clubs."

Relief swamped him. He tried to tell himself it meant nothing, but the truth of it was, he was glad she didn't date around. He hadn't been with anyone other than Chloe. *Ever.* After she'd dumped him, his friends had expected him to rebound, maybe have flings with a few tourists, but he didn't have it in him to use random women to patch up his mangled heart. He had been with Chloe since he was seventeen, so his experience level when it came to women left something to be desired.

"Is it bad if I say I'm glad to hear that?" he asked softly.

Emily shook her head. "No." She nibbled on her lip. "Do you go to the clubs? Spend time with any women?"

"Are you asking me if I'm seeing someone, Em?"

"Maybe."

She looked so nervous of his answer, he chuckled. "No, I'm not. I wouldn't be here with you if I was. I'm old-fashioned like that."

"Good. That's the way I like it."

Her approval warmed him on the inside and being the recipient of her shy smile made him wonder what else he could say to bring it to the fore. He'd never get enough of that smile.

"What about you?" he queried. "Are you seeing anyone?"

"No." He thought she'd leave it at that, but then she huffed out a breath and continued, "I haven't dated anyone more than once since Hemi, two years ago."

Hemi was a great guy. Likable. Justin hadn't known he and Emily dated, but from the outside, they made sense together. "Why didn't it work out?"

Emily shrugged and looked away. "He was too outgoing for me, and I was too much of a workaholic for him. He wanted to spend the weekends surfing or hiking or playing sports, while I wanted to spend it relaxing or building my business. We just didn't gel."

Thank God for that. "Is there a reason you don't date more?"

He knew many women wouldn't answer that question, but curiosity was killing him. Men adored her. Why wasn't she making the most of it? In her shoes, others certainly would have played the field.

"Finding a man isn't high on my priority list."

He winced. So much for romance. "Ouch."

She rolled her eyes. "I didn't mean it like that. I'd be ecstatic if I found Mr. Right. I'm just not actively looking for him."

"Fair enough."

At least she didn't have anything against men. They started walking again, and he kept a hold of her hand. It felt small and breakable compared to his clumsy ones, which were roughened by years of manual labor. He kept his touch soft, afraid of hurting her.

"Do you still care for Chloe?" she asked, all of a sudden.

The question came out of nowhere, although he should have expected it, given that he was at Chloe's wedding. Everyone else here wondered the same thing, they just didn't have the guts to ask. Emily's uncharacteristic directness surprised him, in a good way, and made him wonder: how much did she care about the answer?

"No," he said, rewarding her directness with his own. "I

don't want anything terrible to happen to her, but she proved she wasn't the person I thought she was. After all this time, I can honestly say her betrayal did more damage to my ego than anything else."

"Your ego shouldn't have taken a hit," Emily told him. "You're a handsome, successful man. It's her loss."

And just like that, his head inflated. Emily thought he was handsome. Despite the beard, the outdated clothing, and the fact he should have had a haircut six months ago. He swelled with pride.

As for her other claim... "I think you and Chloe may have different ideas of what 'successful' means." Since his ex had defected Team Justin in favor of Team Rich, he could only assume Chloe preferred a man with a high-paying job and malleable nature.

Emily snorted derisively. "Chloe has a skewed view of the world. Anyone who earns enough to live comfortably, enjoys their job, and is secure in their relationships with others is successful to me."

His hand tightened around hers. "You're a wise woman."

"Don't you forget it."

He checked his watch. Ten to twelve. They'd been wandering outside for quite a while.

"Not long until the countdown," he said. "I think the fireworks are over the other side of the building. You want to head over and wait?"

"Sure." Emily kept her fingers entwined with his as they rejoined the other wedding guests, and it felt like a victory.

AFTER JUSTIN'S confrontation with the guy who'd hit on her, and their conversation in the vineyard, Emily had stumbled upon a shocking truth: he was interested in her. As in, romantically interested. She didn't know how it had happened, or why, but it was impossible to misconstrue his actions. She'd as good as confessed she was interested in him, too. She blushed at the memory. She hadn't intended to say what she had, but she couldn't handle him thinking worse of himself because Satan's Mistress had deserted him.

They stood in the crowd that had assembled to watch the fireworks. The press of bodies kept the chill off the air, but still, she shivered. Her dress didn't cover much.

"Here," Justin said, and warmth surrounded her. His jacket. Heated by his body.

She slid her arms into the sleeves and clutched it tightly around herself. It smelled of him. "Thank you."

Maintaining a rigid spine, she resisted the urge to lean on him at first, but then he shuffled forward so his chest aligned with her back and locked his hands around her waist. She melted into him, letting him take her weight. Being this close to him felt as natural as breathing, but neither of them acknowledged their position, as if afraid the other would run away the second they did. They stayed that way until the countdown began.

"Ten," the crowd chanted. "Nine, eight, seven."

Emily twisted in Justin's arms until she faced him. He was half-hidden by the dark, but his eyes glinted down at her.

"Six, five, four."

Her pulse hammered in her ears and desire licked through her. She wet her lips. Justin twitched in response. This was the moment. Right now, nothing existed but the two of them, wrapped in a bubble of inky darkness.

"Three, two, one."

Starbursts exploded across the sky. Emily stretched onto her tiptoes just as Justin lowered his head. They met halfway. The kiss started gently, both of them testing the water. She breathed him in, loving the scent of him. His beard brushed her lips and cheek. She reached up and curved her palm around his jaw. They parted.

A low growl emanated from Justin's chest, then he claimed her mouth a second time, no longer tentative. His tongue flicked along the seam of her lips, which parted on command.

Their tongues touched, and he groaned, the vibration echoing through her mouth.

Boldly, she stroked his tongue with hers, then sucked. His breath came in ragged gasps. Under the cover of his jacket, he cupped her breast through the dress, then slipped a thumb inside, encountering no resistance. The rough pad of his thumb rubbed back and forth over her nipple, causing thrums of delicious friction, then plucked it into a stiff peak.

"*Justin, not now,*" she gasped, needing him to stop even though she desperately wanted him to continue, wanted him to shove the dress off her shoulders and lavish both of her breasts with attention. But they had to wait. They couldn't do this with an audience.

"Damn," he cursed, breaking away and checking to make sure she was covered. Their foreheads rested against each other as they caught their breath. "You're right," he said. "I know you're right. But wow, that was quite a kiss, Em."

"We should definitely do it again," she agreed. "Just not here."

"You'd want that?" he asked, searching her eyes as if they contained the answers he sought. Though he'd released her, she hadn't backed away, so she could sense when his muscles tightened.

"Yes," she whispered, aware she was opening herself up to rejection. Hopefully that kiss had rocked him as much as it had her.

"Thank you." He kissed her once more, soft and chaste. "For everything. Tonight has been beyond what I expected, thanks to you. Do you even know how special you are?"

She glowed at his praise. "You're special, too."

He laughed, the sound booming in the silence after the fireworks and attracting a few curious glances. "If I'm special, then you must be a goddamn angel."

She thought that might be the nicest compliment anyone had given her.

"Come on, Angel," he said. "Let's get you home."

Justin dreamed of Emily, naked and exposed for his pleasure. In his dream, they didn't stop at a kiss. He didn't drop her off at home, walk her to her door, and leave like a gentleman. Instead, he invited himself in and stripped away all the layers between them, unsatisfied until they'd been wrapped around each other, writhing and sweaty.

Consequently, he had woken bathed in sweat and hard enough to hammer nails. He'd showered, fed his demanding felines—Richie McCat and Dan Catter—named for two of the best rugby players in the world, and headed outside to burn off his frustrated energy. He drove his four-wheeler up a hiking track to a hut and spent a solid two hours chopping and stacking firewood.

Unfortunately, the hard labor didn't distract him from his Emily-related fantasies. Instead, his body fell into the familiar rhythm while his mind wandered, wondering what she looked like under her clothes, whether her skin was the same milky shade everywhere, and whether *all* of her hair was that magnificent shade of red.

As he swung the ax, hearing the thunk of steel into wood, he speculated over what noise she'd make when she came undone. Would she be shy and quiet, or tumble headlong into passion, her generous nature ensuring her lover knew how much she appreciated his effort? He suspected the latter, but desperately wanted to find out for himself. He wanted to hear mewls of arousal spill from her lips, feel her shiver as he touched her, and shudder beneath him as pleasure over-whelmed her.

Fuck, he needed to get himself under control.

With how painfully aroused he was simply at the thought of her, he'd never be able to make her drunk with ecstasy before he lost himself. He returned the ax to the shed and rested a palm on the doorframe, listening. No one was around. The group who'd been staying in the hut had moved on and the next group hadn't arrived yet. Birds chirped in the trees and cicadas hummed in the background. The stream that flowed past the hut bubbled merrily as it made its way down the gentle slope.

He crossed over to the stream and followed it for a hundred yards to where it formed a small pool, not very wide, but deep enough to reach his shoulders. Stripping his clothes off, he laid them on a rock and waded in. The frigid water lapped at his calves. He could have sworn his balls shriveled up as the stream inched up his inner thighs, but he carried on, swearing as it rippled over his sensitive abdomen, the muscles contracting in an attempt to fend off the cold.

He'd known the water would be icy. The stream was formed by glacier melt and stayed much the same temperature year-round, regardless of the warm summer air. He gritted his teeth and ducked beneath the surface. As soon as he fully submerged, he shot back out again and laughed, despite his tingling limbs. The stream had cooled his ardor as effectively as he'd hoped. No hard-on could survive such conditions. The dunk in the pool had also rinsed off the sweat that had accu-mulated on his skin while he'd worked.

Wading out of the pool, he shook off the excess water and

squeezed it out of his hair. He yanked his clothes back on and moisture soaked them instantly, but they'd soon dry out on a day as fine as this one. Before leaving the hut, he checked that the recent visitors had tidied, left payment for using the facilities, and signed the logbook to say where they were going next. Satisfied, he climbed back on his motorcycle and returned home.

Usually, he'd visit another hut, or start a circuit of the traps laid out around the reserve to catch pests—most commonly stoats, which preyed on native birds—but he couldn't focus on anything other than the phenomenal kiss he'd shared with Emily the night before. For months, he'd been attracted to her, but he'd written it off as hopeless infatuation since she'd never showed any sign of returning the attraction. After that kiss, he was confident she felt at least some of the chemistry he did. A kiss like that didn't result from one-sided attraction.

The trouble was, he had zero game. He was a thirty-one-year-old man with minimal dating experience, having been with the same woman since high school. A woman who, incidentally, left him two weeks before their wedding.

What a catch.

But his skills, or lack thereof, didn't matter. There was no need for games. Emily had indicated that she wanted to see him again, so he'd be direct about it. Then she'd be under no illusions that he was capable of grand romantic gestures, and he wouldn't set her up for disappointment in the future. No point putting it off. He'd go to her immediately.

Except… Lifting his arm, he sniffed. A sour odor singed his nose hairs. Okay, he'd change clothes first. He may not know much about dating, but no woman wanted a man who could strip paint with his body odor.

Fifteen minutes later, having showered, deodorized and dressed in a freshly laundered khaki button-down shirt and cargo pants, he drove his old pickup truck into town. Since it was peak tourist season, and Emily's shop was one of the most popular in town, he couldn't find a parking spot nearby, so he settled for parking outside his sister's house and walking into the town center.

Itirangi was bustling, with people crowded outside the bakehouse and Dux restaurant. Others had set up picnics along the shore of the lake, a beautiful blue body of water that stretched towards the mountains on the horizon and was fringed by forest. The lake gave the town its name—Little Sky, in the native Maori tongue.

The number of people around made Justin tense. He preferred Itirangi in the quieter spring and autumn seasons, when there wasn't enough snow on the mountains for the skiing crowd, but it was still too cold for the summer crowd. But the glorious day reminded him of why he loved his home. God, it was beautiful. He'd never lived anywhere else, and he'd never want to. Itirangi was it for him. From the glorious outdoors to the quirky old buildings and peculiar small-town personalities, he adored it all.

Well, almost all of it. He could do without the gossip. It had been ruthless after he and Chloe had broken up. Everywhere he went, people had stopped to stare or express their sympathy with a glint in their eye that let him know him they'd be telling the next person they saw all about poor Jilted Justin. Yeah, he'd heard the nickname. Whispered as he entered a room, murmured behind hands when he turned away. He could admit public sympathy seemed to be on his side, but that didn't make being the subject of gossip any more palatable.

Emily's shop, Pretty Things, looked like her: sweet and feminine. Although he had only been inside a handful of times, he'd noticed how it reflected its owner perfectly. Excitement fluttered in his stomach when the street sign came into view. He couldn't believe how badly he wanted to see her again, to confirm that last night really *had* happened, and that she *was* just as wonderful as he'd imagined.

When he stepped into the shop, he noticed three things:

1. It was crammed full of women;
2. They all turned to stare at him as the doorbell chimed; and
3. Emily was exactly as gorgeous as he'd remembered.

EMILY HUMMED under her breath as she worked on New Year's morning, which was traditionally a busy day for her, being a public holiday. Tourists and locals alike flocked to Main Street and started the year by exploring beautiful Itirangi and all of its temptations. Luckily, her employee Sandra had prepared well yesterday, so the shelves were well stocked, a few popular items discounted, and both of them could spend their time with customers. The doorbell jangled constantly, and each time, Emily glanced up from whatever she was doing and greeted the customer with a smile and a friendly 'hello'.

The busy shop kept her from daydreaming about kissing Justin, which had lived up to her wildest fantasies. So when the bell rang, and she looked up with a smile only to see his bulky frame blocking her doorway, heat spiked her blood and her she forgot whatever she'd been about to say. He came to a sudden stop, eyes widening with something akin to fear at the sight of twenty or so women perusing the store.

Many of the women stopped and ogled him in return. She couldn't blame them. The soft khaki shirt he wore emphasized his thick torso and muscled arms, and his cargo pants displayed tree-trunk thighs. Emily's mouth watered. The beard and wild hair completed the 'sexy outdoorsman' image. He looked ready to throw a woman over his shoulder and carry her off to a rustic cabin in the woods. More than one of her customers fanned themselves.

Justin's eyes widened, the white becoming visible. Emily giggled, then clapped a hand over her mouth. The sharp noise seemed to jolt him into motion. His gaze fixed on her and he shouldered through the throng of women. Without a word, he took her hand and dragged her through the rear exit into her workshop. A laugh died on her lips when he pinned her to the wall, and she felt the delicious press of those muscles she'd admired from a distance.

His eyes searched hers, then his mouth curled upwards in a self-satisfied smile. "Not laughing now, are you?"

She shook her head, unable to speak.

"Good."

He crushed his lips to hers, and all she could do was cling to him and pray he never stopped. Sparks crackled between them and she grabbed fistfuls of his damp hair. White-hot flashes of pleasure flickered across her vision and she closed her eyes, savoring the taste of him in the darkness. Spicy and very, very male.

He yanked free of her, chest heaving as his breath came in puffs. "I like you, Emily."

She couldn't help it. She giggled.

He frowned in confusion. "What's so funny?"

"I've been waiting fifteen years for you to say that." And she'd thought it would never be more than her favorite fantasy.

He blinked at her, as if gathering his thoughts. "You have?"

"You didn't know?" She'd tried to keep her hero worship private, but few things remained secret in Itirangi.

The poor man looked utterly baffled. "Know what?"

Apparently, she'd been a better actress than she'd thought. "I've had a crush on you since I was fourteen," she admitted, watching the play of emotion across his face. "Chloe was picking on me and you told her to stop being a bitch and leave me alone. This was back before you started dating her.'

She could see the moment he remembered.

"She was making fun of your hair," he said.

"And my weight, and my freckles," Emily added. "I was an easy target. I didn't fight back. But you stood up for me."

"And you've been in love with me ever since."

"Hey now, I didn't say that! I had a crush, that was all."

He smiled smugly despite her protestation. "You can deny it all you like, but you want me, Em."

She didn't deny it again. To tell the truth, she enjoyed being responsible for the supremely confident masculine expression he wore, especially after he'd admitted to doubting himself yesterday.

"I do."

He lowered his head to kiss her again. Light and flirty at first, so she could feel him smile against her mouth, but it deepened as she rose on her toes and arched up. She purred contentedly as one of his hands curved around her neck, caressing the hollow of her throat.

She could kiss him like this forever. Forget the customers on the other side of the door. They could make do without her. This was far more important. But as the devil on her shoulder was convincing her to slip out the back and take Justin home with her, someone barged into the workshop and rudely interrupted the best kiss of her life.

"What is it?" Emily demanded breathlessly.

"Sorry, Em," Sandra said from somewhere off to the side. "We need you back out here. I can't keep up with all of these customers."

Burying her face in Justin's chest, Emily sighed. "Okay," she replied, reminding herself that Sandra wasn't personally responsible for her sexual frustration. "I'll be there shortly."

The door clicked shut again. Justin's lips trailed fire down her neck. "I wish you could tell them to go to hell."

She moaned. "So do I."

She pushed his big chest. He moved back, nipping at the crook of her shoulder. His teeth sank into her flesh and scraped gently. The contrast between roughness and tenderness set her pulse racing, and moisture rushed to her core. She'd always craved that hard edge with her pleasure, but she'd never known how to ask for it. Justin seemed to know and instinctively give her what she needed. As if he was made for her. She shivered. If he'd kissed her back when she was four-teen, her crush would have been taken to a whole new level.

"Have dinner at my place tonight," he murmured against her skin. "Please?"

"Yes," she sighed as he licked over the spot he'd bitten, soothing the sting. "What time?"

"Seven o'clock," he replied, stepping back, holding her waist so she didn't fall. Her weak knees would have buckled beneath her weight. Once she was able to stand, he kissed her cheek and said, "See you later, Em."

She waited until he left, then sagged to the ground.

"Oh, my God," she said to herself.

5

She'd said yes. More than that, she'd fallen apart beautifully in Justin's arms when he'd dared to touch her. All of that boded well. So did the fact she hadn't questioned his preference to have their date at his home—out of sight of the gossips. His love life had been the subject of enough gossip without adding fuel to the fire. As he tidied his sparsely furnished living room, he noticed for the first time in months that the cushions on the sofa were worn nearly all the way through and the wooden coffee table in the center of the room was scarred with half a dozen coffee-rings staining the surface.

Damn. Emily was the queen of interior décor. She'd turn her nose up at his home, for sure.

He couldn't do this alone. He needed reinforcements.

"Coop," he said, when his brother answered the phone. "You working?"

"Nope," Cooper replied. "And a good afternoon to you too, bro."

Justin ignored him. Cooper was too much of a smart-alec for his own good.

"I've got a date tonight," he said, without any preamble. "And I don't have a fucking clue what to do."

Cooper laughed at him, the bastard. "Sounds like a dilemma."

"Damn it," Justin grumbled. "Just get your ass down here and help me."

Cooper seemed to think about it. "Will there be beer?"

Justin ran a hand through his hair and tugged on the ends. "I've got a six-pack with your name on it if you're here in less than fifteen minutes."

"See you in ten."

Before Cooper arrived, Justin cleaned up a few superficial things, like the coffee stains, and the layer of dust on basically everything. When Cooper sauntered through the doorway, he beelined to the fridge and opened a bottle of beer. Once he'd taken a long swig, he set the bottle on the counter and jerked his chin up in a nod of greeting.

"You got a date, huh?" he asked. "Been long enough."

Justin grunted. "Tell me about it. I haven't had a first date since high school."

"Who's the lucky girl?"

Justin hesitated. "Promise me Mum and Dad won't hear about this. It's one date, not a relationship."

Yet. It'd be a relationship before long, if everything went according to plan.

Cooper spun circles with his finger. "My word is my bond, yada yada. Get on with it. I want to know who's pulled you out of that misery pit of despair that Chloe cast you into."

"I haven't been that bad," Justin muttered, a little miffed. So he hadn't been the leader of the cheer squad lately. He'd hardly been Scrooge either. "It's Emily."

Cooper raised an eyebrow. "Little Miss Sunshine." He shook his head slowly. "You asked Emily Parker on a date and she said *yes?*"

Crossing his arms defensively, Justin scowled. "You don't have to make it sound like I'm a beast or something."

Recalling the way Emily's breath had come in soft little gasps when he'd kissed her and how she'd blushed prettily when she admitted she'd had a crush on him in high school, he didn't think she had a problem with his looks.

She'd had a crush on him.

When she'd told him that, he'd felt manlier than he had in months. Years, even. How could a woman like Emily desire a man like him, when, in his typical idiotic fashion, he'd over-looked her? He could have spent years with Emily rather than Chloe, but he'd been like all teenage boys, flattered by the attention of a self-confident girl.

"Earth to Justin."

He snapped to attention.

"Where'd you go, man?"

He shrugged and didn't reply. Cooper surveyed him from head to toe, and suddenly he was very aware of his unfashionable clothes and scruffy appearance, which was exaggerated in comparison to his brother's golden good looks, low-slung jeans and leather jacket.

"I say this lovingly," Cooper began. "You're a fixer-upper, and Emily's notoriously slippery. Manages to avoid dating anyone without blatantly turning them down. So it surprises me she'd make an exception for you."

Which made it vital he not screw this up. "If you're done insulting me, can you tell me how to make sure she comes back for a second date?"

Cooper lifted one shoulder. "I don't think my advice is going to help you."

Justin's heart sunk. "Is it a hopeless case?"

His brother sighed. "You would take that comment the wrong way, wouldn't you? You're your own worst enemy. What I meant is that Emily has rejected me and most of the guys I know at some time or other, but she said yes to you and what I'm sure was the most unromantic dinner invitation ever, so I've got no idea what makes her tick. I could try to teach you my moves, but I doubt they'd do you any good." He clapped Justin on the back. "Apparently, she likes you, bro. Just thank your lucky stars and be yourself."

"Worst advice ever," Justin grouched.

"Best I can do," Cooper said. "But there's one other piece of advice I can offer: pretty this place up a bit. Come on, it screams 'I don't give a damn'. Women don't like that. Get some candles or flowers. Vacuum." He picked fluff from his pants. "There's cat fur on everything."

"I could have figured that out myself."

"So why ask me for help?"

Justin paused. He didn't really know. Lack of self-assurance, probably. But he'd come this far on his own. He just needed to believe in himself. And in Emily. She wasn't shallow enough to dismiss him because he lacked the polish of some men. Heck, maybe she was even attracted to him *because* of that.

He could do this.

"I'm being a dumbass, aren't I?"

"Yes. Amen to that." Cooper finished his beer, grabbed the rest of the box and headed for the door. "I've gotta get home. Got some photos to develop. Trust your gut and for God's sake, don't mention Chloe. Oh," he paused in the doorway, "and try to smile. The moody, brooding thing is so five years ago."

Justin stretched his lips into a grimace, exposing his teeth.

Cooper looked taken aback. "On second thought, maybe don't smile. You'll scare her off."

"Thanks, man."

Cooper saluted. "No worries. Let me know how it goes. And change your sheets, just in case."

The door swung shut behind him. Justin pondered his parting comment. *Change the sheets.*

He shouldn't. It would be presumptuous. Emily wasn't that

kind of girl. But it *had* been two weeks since he'd washed them. What could it hurt?

A quick trip into Timaru, the nearest city, to buy a few candles and a tablecloth—he couldn't risk buying them in Itirangi, the old biddies would be swapping stories about it within the hour—and he returned home for a tidying spree. He didn't buy flowers. Buying flowers for a talented florist seemed like too great of a risk. What if he chose the wrong ones?

For dinner, he opted to cook a barbecue, because frankly, it was the only thing he trusted himself not to screw up. Richie and Dan watched with interest and what seemed like a healthy portion of judgment. The bloody cats were always looking down their noses at him. And yet he tossed them each a treat and petted them as they twined around his legs. They were a damn nuisance, but a man couldn't deny they were cute.

As she knocked on the door of Justin's charming timber house, which was set back from the highway heading out of Itirangi, amongst the trees, Emily rethought her outfit for the umpteenth time. She hadn't gone on a date she really cared about in years and her nerves made her question everything. If they were going to a restaurant, she'd have an idea of what dress code was appropriate, but at Justin's home, she had no baseline knowledge to guide her decision. She wanted to knock him off his feet, but he was a low-key guy, and if she overdid it, he might think her too high maintenance. On the flipside, if she dressed down, she risked losing his interest, so she'd settled for a mint green dress with strappy black sandals and a swipe of lip gloss and mascara. Feminine, but understated.

Unsure of the correct etiquette, she had umm-ed and aah-ed over whether to bring anything. She'd considered wine, but Justin didn't strike her as a wine guy. She thought about buying dessert from the bakehouse but didn't know what his tastes ran to. In the end, she'd purchased a small box of chocolate pralines from her friend Kayla's artisan chocolate shop. No one could say no to Kayla's chocolates. They were made with love.

When the door swung inward, Justin greeted her with a kiss on the cheek and Emily's jaw dropped. In half a day, he'd undergone quite a transformation. His hair had been trimmed and his scruffy beard tamed until it looked less caveman, more Jason Momoa. Hot as hell.

Her gaze tracked down his body, noting dark jeans and a short-sleeved button-down shirt. It seemed he had gone all-out. She hadn't seen him look so put together since Chloe left him. A warm glow grew within her. He'd made a special effort. Even at the wedding yesterday he'd been scruffy, but he'd tidied up for her.

"You trimmed your beard," she said. He nodded, touching it self-consciously. "And you're wearing a nice shirt."

He cleared his throat. "I am."

She smiled. "You look good."

"So do you. Like always. Come in."

She followed him into the living room, which featured a sofa, an armchair, and a coffee table, all in shades of brown. The bare walls were painted cream and the carpet was gray. A TV was affixed to the wall facing the sofa. Very utilitarian. Missing splashes of color. A woman's touch. If she lived here, she'd frame photos and hang them on the walls, complement them with a painting, and add colored throws, mats, and cushions to bring some life to the place. A person's surroundings affected their mood, and Justin's home needed some brightness.

Don't get ahead of yourself.

At the moment, his furnishings were none of her business. There might come a time when they were, but she needed to slow down. A black cat lay curled on the armchair and a fluffy tabby butted his head against her leg. She bent to pat him.

"That's Dan," Justin told her. "The one on the couch is

Richie. They're a nuisance, but they're decent ratters, so I keep them around."

"Unique names for cats," she remarked, scratching Dan behind his ear, pleased when he purred in response.

"Named for Carter and McCaw," Justin explained.

"Of course." He'd named his cats after legendary rugby players. She wouldn't expect anything less from a rabid All Blacks fan. "Cute."

He glanced at the cats. "I wouldn't know. I only care how many rats they kill."

But the way he picked up Richie and draped him over his shoulder before opening the French door on the far side of the living room made a liar of him. Emily hid a smile. The fact he didn't want her to know what a softie he was only made him more adorable. He could speak in a gruff voice and deny it all he wanted, but a man who wore his cat as a scarf loved that cat to bits.

"Out here," he said, gesturing for her to join him. When she did, she heard sizzling and followed her nose to the barbecue on his lawn, situated beside a picnic table upon which three candles were burning.

"What's on the barbie?" she asked.

"Mushrooms and onions so far, but we're having steak, too. That okay?"

"Steak is great."

He put the cat down and added two steaks to the grill. "How would you like it done?"

"Medium is good, thanks."

Sitting at the picnic table, Emily crossed her ankles. The fresh scent of earth and trees hung in the air, woodsy and relaxing. The backyard was an oasis of lawn amongst the forest, with no gardens or paths. Simple and masculine, much like the interior of the house. Birds called in trees, out of sight. Despite the hour, it was still daylight. She tilted her head back to look at the blue sky. A cloud floated across her vision.

"What a beautiful place to live," she said. "I'm quite jealous."

Justin checked the mushrooms and onions. The aroma made her salivate.

"You live in town, don't you?" he asked.

"Yeah. A few houses down from Aria."

Emily's place was nice, but she'd always intended it to be temporary. A stopgap until she found somewhere she liked better. Then she'd gotten busy with work and finding a permanent home had slipped down her to-do list.

Justin flipped the steaks then went inside and came back with two bowls of salad: potato and lettuce.

Emily laughed delightedly. "You've got the barbecue meal down to an art."

"It's the one form of cooking I've mastered," he replied, eyes crinkling at the corners. "So don't expect too much from me on the second date."

She liked the lines around his eyes and the faint brackets around his mouth. They showed he smiled often—or at least, he had at some point in time. They also showed that he was a man, not a boy. He'd lived enough to know who he was and what he wanted. And apparently, he wanted her. Enough for a second date, at least.

"How about I cook next time?" she suggested.

His eyes widened, as if she'd surprised him. "I'd like that. It's a date. Provided you want to see me again after tonight," he added wryly as he loaded steak, mushrooms and onions onto plates and carried them to the table, sitting opposite her.

"Justin," she said dryly, "we live in a tiny town. Even if we didn't go on another date, we'd see each other again. The perils of being in Itirangi."

"Thanks for the reminder."

They each dished up dinner and settled in. Justin had indeed mastered the barbecue; Emily's steak was perfect. While they ate, they talked. Well, mostly Emily talked, but when Justin chimed in, she found herself laughing and feeling giddier than she had since high school when she'd watched him across the classroom. She wondered what could possess any woman to throw away his affection. When their cutlery clattered against empty plates, he put his weight on his elbows and leaned across the table toward her.

"I know this is when I'm supposed to play it cool," he said, "but I really want to go on another date with you, Em. I'm not the kind of guy who plays games. I think we could have something special, and I want to see where it goes."

Her heart thundered so loud she could hardly hear him over the sound of it.

"I'd love it if you came back tomorrow," he continued. "Same time, same place. If you'd like to cook, I can stock the kitchen with whatever you need."

"I…uh…" She thought she'd become immune to bluntness, but when Justin gazed into her eyes and said things like that, it challenged her sanity. What girl wouldn't love to be the subject of his single-minded focus? "You don't need to stock the kitchen," she said. "I'll bring over everything I need."

Her cheesy pasta bake could win any man's heart.

"So, that's a yes?"

She lifted from the seat and closed some of the distance between them. "That's a yes," she confirmed.

He seized her face and kissed her, upending the bowl of potato salad. He cursed and started to pull back, but she gripped his shirt and yanked him closer.

"Ignore it," she murmured against his mouth.

Their tongues entwined, and she didn't care that she was awkwardly splayed across a table, or that her breath probably smelled of onions, because this was *Justin* kissing her. *Justin*, who she'd wanted forever. If she could imprint this moment on her memory, she would.

Hours later, she still tasted his kiss on her lips.

---

6

*R*ather than cook at Justin's place, Emily prepared dinner ahead of time and packed it in a Tupperware container. Tonight, she was a woman with a plan, and wasting time in his kitchen didn't figure into it. Tonight, she was going to seduce him.

Enough was enough. Thus far, his kisses and teasing touches had led nowhere, so it fell to her to take their relationship to the next level. She'd visited the lingerie store during her lunch break and purchased a sheer negligee and matching underwear.

In addition to the negligee, she also packed clean clothes and toiletries, hoping she wasn't being overly optimistic. Wearing a short dress over the lingerie, she drove to Justin's house half an hour early because she simply couldn't wait any longer and marched to the door, leaving everything other than dinner in her car. She'd come back for it later. *After.* Letting herself inside, she put dinner in the fridge and went looking for him. A short hall extended from the living room, with three rooms adjoining it. One of those doors opened and she stopped abruptly at the sight of a mostly naked male torso.

Holy moly.

If God ever created a man in his image, Justin Simons was it: built, masculine, uncompromising. Her eyes alighted on the wall of muscle that was his chest. Firm pectorals, prominent trapezoids, and strong deltoids. She longed to trace the edge of the pecs with her fingertip and then beneath, to the ridges of his abdomen and further to where a deep vee grooved from the bottom of his obliques into the towel wrapped around his hips.

He straightened, hands on hips, arms bulging. Best of all, dark ink swirled around his shoulder in knots and twists. Emily's mouth watered, and she promised herself, before the night was out, she'd follow the lines of that tattoo with her tongue.

"I was in the shower. Didn't hear you arrive," he said, making no move to cover himself. Water dripped from the tips of his damp hair onto his shoulders

"I let myself in," she replied. "I hope that's okay."

Then, since he was already halfway to being naked and it seemed like an appropriate time, she stripped her dress off. It pooled at her feet, and now it was Justin's turn to stare. She held her head high and refused to waver. She knew the ruby-red negligee suited her skin tone and left most of her exposed. She hoped he liked what he saw. Based on his hungry expression, she'd say he did.

WHEN EMILY REMOVED HER DRESS, Justin's capacity for rational thought fled.

She was perfect. An angel of seduction.

The red lacy thing she wore alternately concealed and revealed, following the contours of her curves, dipping into the hollow between her breasts, presenting her for his enjoyment like a succulent, gift-wrapped present. One he wanted to unwrap inch by inch.

"You're so fucking gorgeous," he said, feasting on her with his eyes. "Can I just look at you for a while?"

He needn't have worried that she'd be too shy—she let him look his fill.

"Twirl for me," he ordered.

Torturously slowly, she spun in a circle so he could see her from every side. What he saw only reinforced his initial impression. *Perfect.*

"Take it off."

She pulled a ribbon tied in a bow above her cleavage and the fabric fell away, leaving her in a red thong and nothing else. *Jesus.* Her aureoles were pale peach, as he'd suspected. Her skin tone was even, as if she bathed in milk every day like Queen Cleopatra. In contrast, his own skin was marred by tan lines and patches of sunburn.

He'd wondered previously whether she'd have freckles, but except for an apricot-colored spot on her breast and another on her collarbone, she was free of blemishes. Surprising, given her coloring.

"I hope you're sure about this," he said, afraid to lay his greedy hands on her lest she have second thoughts. He wasn't sure he could survive the frustration if she did.

"I'm sure," she replied without hesitation. "I promise. And if you're sure, too, I'd really appreciate it if you'd return the favor and get out of that towel."

Bossy like a queen, too. A smile quirked his lips. Damn if he didn't like her spunk.

He dropped the towel and kicked it to the side, now standing in only his briefs. "Better?" he demanded.

She pursed her lips, flicked a glance down to rest on his crotch, which throbbed in response to her scrutiny, then shook her head. "Still too many clothes."

The laugh that boomed from his chest startled both of them. But while Emily's brow furrowed with concern, Justin's heart lightened. There had never been laughter between him and Chloe during moments of intimacy. Already, things with Emily were better and they weren't even naked yet.

She had laid down the gauntlet. He responded by shaking off his underwear and posing for her, flexing his biceps and tensing his abs, his erection jutting out proudly as if trying to get closer to the source of its excitement. When it came to his body, he was confident bordering on arrogant. While he may overlook personal grooming from time to time, his physically demanding job ensured he was fitter than many gym junkies.

"Happy now?"

"Hmm." Emily stared at him, looking equal parts fascinated and nervous.

That's right, sweetheart. This will be inside you real soon.

He could lose his head just thinking about it. In the past, he had suppressed his dirtiest fantasies because he thought that was what Chloe wanted, but the way Emily had reacted to his rough kisses and manhandling over the last couple of days made him optimistic he wouldn't have to rein in his impulses like he had before. That possibility only excited him further.

You can't afford to get this wrong, he reminded himself. He had to make it so earth-shatteringly good for her that she became addicted to him and accepted she couldn't get the same pleasure from anyone else.

Emily swallowed apprehensively, and a flicker of doubt splashed like icy water down his spine. He hadn't been able to please Chloe enough to keep her around, and he hadn't tried with another woman since. What if he failed with Emily, too?

He shut down the thought. Failure wasn't an option.

"Stop thinking," Emily said, as if she could hear the cacophony of voices arguing in his head.

He was about to say he couldn't just switch them off when she lowered her thong so she was totally naked before him. And then, he discovered he could indeed switch them off, given sufficient distraction.

"COME HERE," Justin growled, low and gravelly.

Even his voice made Emily wet. She went to him. To her surprise, when he reached for her, his hands landed in strictly PG locations. He cupped her face and anchored her to him with a hand on her hip. Then he kissed her.

As with their New Year's kiss, it started sweet and soft, but when Justin scraped his teeth over her bottom lip, she moaned and rocked into him and the kiss heated quickly, becoming a gnash of tongues and teeth. They tasted each other, boldly stroking and licking. He nipped at her mouth, pinching her full lower lip between his teeth then running his tongue along its length. The contrast between the gentlemanly way he held her and the crude plundering of her mouth made her desperate for him to do the same thing all over her body. She wanted him to lick and bite and love every inch of her.

"Touch me," she begged, sounding breathless and reckless, totally unlike herself.

"How do you want to be touched?" he asked, burying his face in the crook of her shoulder, his beard rough against her skin. He nuzzled her gently, tongue darting out to taste her collarbone. He found the spot where he'd bitten her the day before, clamped his teeth on it and sucked. Not hard enough to hurt, but hard enough for her to know he'd leave a mark.

She whimpered and clasped him tightly to her, searching for pressure to ease the ache between her legs. She loved the idea of him marking her, then after he was gone, she'd see the marks and remember all of the filthy, wonderful things they'd done together.

"Like that," she murmured. "Just like that. But please, I need your hands on me. Everywhere. All over."

The hand on her neck burned a trail of fire down her body to join the other. He gripped her butt cheeks and squeezed, his fingers sinking into the soft flesh. He guided her along the length of his erection, the blunt head dragging through her slick folds, then crushed her to his pelvis. Her head fell back and her mouth opened on a gasp as pleasure jolted through her, sudden and intense.

"You like that," he rasped, watching her face intently.

She barely managed to nod. He closed his eyes and slid her back along his erection, and she cried out.

"You like me being rough. Aw, hell, Em. You're so perfect." He rocked their bodies together and breath hissed between his teeth. "So perfect for me." Something scraped the back of her thighs. The bed. "Lie down, sweetheart," he said. "Legs apart. Open yourself for me."

She lay back, then took a hold of her knees and drew them to the sides, leaving herself exposed and vulnerable. For a long moment he just looked at her, and she wondered what he was thinking. It was impossible to tell what was going on behind those near-black eyes. Before she could ask, he knelt and lowered his mouth.

She squeaked in shock. He caught her eyes and smiled wickedly. Using his mouth and lips, he teased her into a mindless state of need, then slipped a finger inside her and crooked it. As he did, his tongue flicked her, and she shuddered, breasts heaving. He did it again, then added a second finger, stretching her until she felt full. Good God, if his fingers devastated her like this, how would she ever survive sex?

She kept her eyes on him, and the sensations he created were made all the more erotic by seeing his mouth on her, watching his fingers plunge into her body. When he twisted his hand and pressed down on her, stars exploded behind her eyes and her body went limp.

∽

Justin had never seen anything as mesmerizing as Emily when she came. First, her eyes squeezed shut, then her entire body shook, and finally his name passed her trembling lips and she collapsed.

She entranced him.

"Emily," he murmured. "Sweetheart, how do you feel?"

Her eyelids fluttered, her irises now a deep moss color as she studied him from beneath her lashes. "Wonderful," she replied softly. "That was beyond amazing. I never dreamed…"

Satisfaction roared through him, and he felt like a king. "You liked it?"

"I more than liked it." She blinked, the haziness in her eyes lifting, and smiled saucily. "Now it's my turn."

He didn't have to wonder what she meant for long She sat up and pulled him onto the bed with her, then straddled his legs. Her slender fingers wrapped around his length and she moistened her lips. He pulsed helplessly in her palm, liquid beading at the tip. Oh, God. He couldn't… She couldn't… She started to lower her head.

"No!" he gasped, yanking free of her.

She frowned and reached for him again. "Why not? You had your fun."

He groaned. "In case you haven't noticed, I'm wound pretty tight, sweetheart. I need to make this good for you, but if you play with me like you want to, I won't be able to do that. You can play later." God, he hoped she would. He'd love to have her hot mouth on him, but not as much as he *needed* to get inside her.

He shifted her to the side, rolled away, grabbed a condom and sheathed himself, then returned and caged her between his arms, holding himself up so he wouldn't crush her. He tested her with his blunt head.

"You're so wet," he said tightly. "So ready for me."

He eased in, an inch at a time. He was thick and the last thing he wanted was to hurt her, but then she grasped his ass and thrust upwards, impaling herself on him. His head spun.

Her narrow channel clasped him tight and pleasure built at the base of his spine.

Shit. Get yourself under control, man.

He couldn't come in two thrusts like a chump kid. He had to get her there first. Luckily, he was learning what made her hot. He claimed her mouth with luscious, carnal kisses, dragging her deep into the storm of sensation with him. He nipped the end of her tongue, then licked it better. She clamped around him. He hooked his arm under her leg and drew her knee up so he had better access to her. Then he drove into her with long, satisfying thrusts.

"I love it when you do that," she gasped, rolling her hips to meet him.

Her breaths came quickly, her beautiful breasts bouncing with each thrust. The pressure at the base of his spine grew. He gritted his teeth. Even his wildest fantasies didn't come close to this. Emily was a mass of contradictions, his sweet angel with a wild side. If other men saw her this way, they'd be queuing up for miles to vie for her affection.

The thought of her with other men was like a stab in the gut. Desperate to assert his control, he dropped her leg and pressed his palm into her arousal. She bucked against his hand, but he held firm. Her head thrashed from side to side, eyes closed, desperate for the release only *he* could give her.

"That's right, Em," he encouraged. "Come for me. I want to see you come again."

He'd become a voyeur, getting off on witnessing her pleasure. He needed it. Was greedy for any sign of her approval. She moaned and spasmed around him. The moment before she drew him over the edge, her eyes opened and captured him as he emptied into her with a hoarse shout.

7

*E*mily snuggled into Justin's side. He hugged her with one arm and nuzzled the top of her head. Tilting her face up, she kissed his lips. The frantic need from earlier had seeped away and she was boneless and sated, enjoying the way he held her close as if he couldn't bear to be parted from her. Using his chest as a pillow, she rubbed her cheek against his rough hair and smiled. Happiness fizzed through her, bubbling up her throat and emerging as a joyful laugh.

"What's going on in that head of yours?" he asked, the vibrations tickling her ear.

"Nothing," she replied, smiling. "I'm just happy."

"Me, too," he agreed. "You make me happy." A moment later, he added, "I can't believe you seduced me. Sweet little Emily Parker. No one would ever believe it."

"Not so sweet," she said, "and I haven't been little in years."

"You're little compared to me."

"*Everyone* is little compared to you."

Justin chuckled. She loved the deep, throaty sound of it. He didn't laugh often enough for her liking. If he let her, she'd make him laugh every day for the rest of his life. Not that she'd let on yet how much he meant to her. For all she knew, she could be a rebound to him.

"Can't argue with that," he said.

His stomach growled loudly, and Emily patted it. "Um, I think it might be time to feed you."

"Nah, I want to snuggle." He rolled them onto their sides, spooning her, making her feel cherished and protected. The way she felt right then, she'd do anything for him.

His stomach growled again. Violently.

"You need food," she said firmly. "I'll heat up dinner. Stay here."

Extricating herself from him, which took a little effort since he refused to cooperate, she padded out to the kitchen naked. After all, out here in the country, surrounded by trees, no one could see her. She dished up two bowls of pasta bake and heated them in the microwave, then returned to Justin's bedroom. One of the cats—Dan, she thought—had curled into a ball on Justin's stomach. She placed the bowls on a cupboard, lifted the cat off, handed Justin a bowl and slid under the covers next to him.

"Smells good," Justin said, eating with gusto.

Emily watched the fork fly from bowl to mouth and back in amazement. In less than two minutes, the bowl was empty.

"Would you like more?" she asked. Thankfully, the recipe was intended to serve four.

"There's more?" he asked like an eager puppy.

She nodded. "In the fridge."

"I'll sort it out," he said, pushing the blankets back. "You eat."

By the time he came back, Emily had consumed enough that she was no longer hungry, so she set her bowl aside. She didn't want to stuff herself because then she wouldn't be prepared for round two of sex. And provided Justin was game, she was keen for round two.

After he'd munched down his second bowl, he crawled over her body and settled between her legs. "Time for dessert."

"Yes," she agreed. And she wasn't talking about the chocolates.

THE NEXT MORNING, Justin slept deeply, not waking when Emily dressed and made coffee, or when she left a steaming mug on his bedside cabinet. She strolled through the house, exploring, though there wasn't much to explore. Everywhere she went, she encountered the same soul-crushing monochromatic color scheme.

She opened the curtains to let light into the house, except for in the bedroom where Justin was dozing. The light that filtered through the windows was weak, as they were covered by a film of dust. Searching in the laundry cupboards, she found a cloth and glass cleaner and wiped down the windows in the living room, kitchen, and bathroom so early morning sun illuminated the rooms. Hands on hips, she studied her work, then smiled. This had to brighten Justin's day. Sunlight was the primary source of vitamin D, which recent studies had linked to positive mood. More vitamin D equaled a better mood. It was science.

Unfortunately, the sun highlighted speckles of dust on the coffee table, vanity and kitchen bench. She searched for a clean cloth to clear off the dust, then fetched a few items she'd brought over from the shop last night out of her car. Collecting them in her arms, she staggered inside and laid them on the couch. Amongst the items were a green glass vase, which she'd thought would suit Justin's preference for the outdoors, a bouquet of wildflowers, two buttery yellow cushions for the sofa, and lastly, a wall hanging depicting a mountainous landscape against a brilliant blue sky.

Choosing the right things to perk up Justin's house had been difficult, and she hoped she hadn't messed up, but if she had, she could always take the rejects to her own home and try again. What was most important was that his home felt right to him.

She wondered how he'd react when he noticed her additions. Hopefully, it would be a pleasant surprise. Something to bring a smile to his face. Being the kind of guy he was, Justin probably had no clue how to make the most of his living space. Fortunately for him, she was an expert.

She peeled the plastic wrapping from the bouquet, filled the bottom of the vase with water, and slotted the flowers into it before placing the vase in the center of the coffee table. Then, in a stroke of genius, she arranged wrapped chocolate pralines in a circle around the base of the vase. She plumped the cushions on the sofa and searched for somewhere to hang the mountain scene. A nail extended from the wall a couple of yards to the left of the TV so she hung it from that. Better to make use of the existing nail, which she assumed had previously held some kind of artwork, than to hammer in a new one and wake Justin up.

Gazing around, she weighed her efforts. She'd only added a few touches of color, but already the atmosphere had lightened. It actually looked like someone lived here, and the cave-like darkness had receded. She nodded to herself. She'd done well.

Detouring to the bedroom, she bent to kiss Justin's cheek. His muscles were slack with sleep, but he mumbled something as she kissed him.

"I'm going now," she whispered. "I've got to open the shop."

"Come back tonight," he said, eyes still closed. "Promise."

"I will," she agreed, and then left, feeling lighter than air, as if she could stretch her arms and fly. She already wanted to see him again. The day couldn't pass quickly enough.

J USTIN'S first clue that something was off was when he wandered from the bedroom into the living room, rubbed his bleary eyes, and froze at the sight of an enormous white and blue picture occupying the wall opposite the hall. The space where the photo of him and Chloe taken on the day of their engagement used to hang. He peered at the picture through narrowed eyes. Where had it come from? The damn thing had to be four feet tall and just as wide. It dominated the wall, detracting attention from the TV. Unfortunately, it also reminded him of Chloe, simply by virtue of its location. In a moment of clarity, he realized where it had come from. *Emily.* Almost as though she'd zeroed in on a vulnerable spot and tried to make it her own.

Looking away from the painting on the wall, Justin's gaze landed on a pair of yellow cushions on the sofa which he'd certainly not put there. Purple and white flowers graced the coffee table. Cold sliced through him. Emily meant well, he knew she did. But hell, she'd spent one night with him and already she was trying to change his home. Change *him.* That didn't bode well for the future. He sucked in a deep breath and released it. He could handle this. He liked Emily, and they were combustible between the sheets.

Don't panic.

He had a woman in his life again. Adjustments were neces-sary. He could adapt. It was only a couple of minor changes. No biggie.

A FTER ANOTHER SATISFYING night spent tangled in the sheets with his woman, Justin stretched, opened his eyes, and jerked back at the sight of a rustic wooden clock on the wall facing the bed. A clock that hadn't been there the previous night. It looked like a slice taken from a tree trunk with grooves etched into it to represent the hours and two simple black hands.

He considered the clock. It suited his style. If he'd wanted a clock, he may well have chosen this one for himself, but the fact was, he *intentionally* didn't have a clock in his bedroom because he didn't want to feel rushed in the morning. Sure, he usually rose early—by his standards, if not Emily's—but if he decided to engage in a leisurely sleep-in, he preferred not to be reminded of the time passing. The bedroom was a place to relax.

Apparently, Emily didn't get that.

He closed his eyes, dug the heel of his palms into his eye sockets, and groaned. Was this her way of hinting that he should be getting up earlier? Making more of his day? Who the hell knew? What he did know was that he couldn't tolerate this change, so he dragged himself out of bed, lifted the clock from the wall and took it to the living room, where he placed it on the windowsill.

Once again, he noticed that the curtains had been opened and the glass cleaned. He couldn't decide whether he appreciated Emily's efforts, or resented them.

"She means well," he repeated to himself. He'd have to talk to her about it sometime. Just, not right now. For a little while longer, he wanted to revel in their budding relationship. In the way she felt in his arms. So perfect. So right.

EMILY WOKE with a muscular arm draped over her waist, curled beneath the front of her hip. She smiled a blissful smile and snuggled back into Justin's chest. His arm tightened around her and he nuzzled the nape of her neck.

"Good morning," she murmured, enjoying the warmth of him wrapped around her.

"Mornin', sweetheart," he rumbled, his voice raspy with sleep.

She wriggled and felt him harden against her butt. Her eyes

flew open. Uh-oh. She tried to extricate herself from him, but he only held tighter.

"Don't start something you're not prepared to finish," he said, his palm skimming up her side to cup her breast.

"I need to get to work," she replied, breathless. Although maybe-kinda-sorta she wouldn't mind him making her late. But he sighed heavily and released her. She slid out from the bed, dressed—she'd shower at her place on the way—and pressed a soft kiss to his lips, then the tip of his nose, and finally his forehead. A surge of affection welled in her heart. She already felt so much for her gorgeous, grumpy man.

She glanced up at the wall to check the time but noticed the clock she'd hung had been moved. That didn't dishearten her. Quite the contrary, it demonstrated that Justin was okay with the other changes she'd made around the place. Clearly, he wouldn't hesitate to make it known if she crossed a line. She'd made a mistake with the clock. That was okay. Mistakes happened. She hummed as she unloaded her latest acquisitions, wondering what he'd think. They certainly made *her* feel more at home. Five minutes later, she departed with a satisfied smile on her face

JUSTIN COULD TEAR his hair out.

Each time Emily visited, something new appeared in his house. A painting of Lake Itirangi on the wall. A jar of cookies on the bench. A 'welcome home' mat on the front doorstep. He'd tolerated it all with nothing more than a raised eyebrow, then whisked her into the bedroom. None of it had been worth starting an argument over. The clock had been easy enough to move, and he'd seen how she could imagine he'd like it, but this time she'd gone too far.

He had stepped into the bathroom, lifted the seat on the toilet—which he didn't mind doing, for the record—only to glance down and notice the pink fluff that squished between his toes.

Pink. Fluff.

Emily had installed a fluffy pink mat at the foot of his toilet, and when he lowered the lid to flush, he noticed a matching cover on the cistern.

Fuck no.

He was a *man*, damn it. He couldn't have fluffy pink covers on his toilet. Not for anyone, not even Emily. And what was she thinking, bringing it here? They may be seeing each other, but they hadn't discussed their relationship status—which meant, as far as he was concerned, that she had no reason to deck out his place in pink stuff. She had no right to try to change his house or try to change *him*.

What a mess.

He raked a hand through his hair, tugging at the ends. Everything had spiraled rapidly out of control, and it was his own stupid fault. He'd been caught up in being with Emily, and not doing anything to put her off, but he needed to look at the facts.

Fact: he didn't need to be changed.

Fact: he definitely didn't need a fluffy pink mat in the bathroom.

Fact: Emily was making changes in his life that he hadn't asked for and didn't want.

Fact: he needed to nip the problem in the bud. Immediately.

8

"*E*mily, I can't stay quiet any longer. You've gone a step too far this time."

Emily held the phone away and stared at it, stunned. Justin's voice was low, but undeniably annoyed. Warily, she returned the phone to her ear.

"A few bits and pieces was okay, but I can't handle a pink abomination in my bathroom"

She cringed, his frustrated tone summoning memories of hiding in her bedroom while her mother and father argued on the other side of the door. Of lying on the floor, hiding while her mum berated her dad for not fixing the sink fast enough, or allowing the dog to put its muddy paws on the sofa. Apparently, Justin didn't like her most recent addition to his home.

She was tempted to close her eyes and stick her fingers in her ears, but this wasn't the end of the world, and she couldn't hide from it. She'd overdone it, but at least now she knew where he drew the line. She'd known the rug was a risk, but it had felt so soft under her feet and he hadn't seemed to mind the other additions to the house—had even remarked on how nice it was to have cookies available whenever he wanted, and how the new scented diffuser in the bathroom smelled like vanilla. She'd thought she was brightening up his home as she'd set out to do, making it a nicer place to live. Surely, he would have said something if he'd been unhappy.

It would seem not.

"Hold on," she said to him, then she turned to Sandra, who was conversing with a customer. "I need to take this call somewhere private. Are you all right out here?"

"Yes, we're good. Take as much time as you need."

With a straight spine, Emily walked to the workshop. Memories of her time in here with Justin assailed her but she did her best to ignore them and focus on the here and now. As soon as the door clicked shut, she sank to the ground.

"I'm back," she told him. "I'm sorry about the rug. I'll get rid of it tonight."

He sighed, sounding wound up. "This isn't just about the rug."

She drew her knees up to her chest and hugged them for comfort. While he wasn't yelling or swearing, she didn't handle conflict of any kind well. She tended to crumple the moment anyone raised their voice.

"What is it about, then?"

"It's..." He seemed to struggle to find the words. "First the flowers, the massive picture on the wall, and now a rug? It's gotta stop, Em. My place was fine the way it was."

"I was just trying to help," she whispered, her voice wobbling.

"That's not how it feels," he said. "It feels like you're trying to change me. But I don't want that, and I don't need another woman who makes me pretend to be something I'm not."

Emily sniffed, tears leaking down her face. Though she'd heard of his hot temper—everyone had—he'd never been growly with her, and she didn't know how to respond. But what really made her heart ache was the fact he honestly believed she didn't adore him the way he was.

"I don't want to change you," she said so quietly she barely heard herself. He paused to listen. "I like you the way you are."

He snorted derisively. "You've got a funny way of showing it."

"I'm sorry," she apologized, wiping her cheeks with the heel of her hand. She had to explain, to make him understand. But in the face of his unhappiness, she couldn't think straight let alone utter the words that would make him forgive her. Her mouth worked, and no sound came out.

"I don't know if I can do this," he said. "I thought I was ready for another relationship, but maybe I'm not. Maybe I won't ever be."

Wait—was he breaking up with her? She slapped one palm to the floor to ground herself, then shifted and lowered her forehead to the wall, the coolness bringing the room back into focus, although it remained blurry at the edges, courtesy of the blood rushing to her head. Everything was moving so fast. How had this escalated so rapidly?

"I'll take it all away, I promise." Words spewed from her mouth, and she thanked her lucky stars that her lunch didn't also spew forth. Once, in primary school, a teacher had publicly chastised her, and she'd thrown up on his boots. She'd been taunted with the nickname 'Pukey Parker' for years.

"I won't bring any more over," she added. "I don't want to change you, and I'm so, so sorry if it seemed that way. I'd never want you to feel that way. Please believe me."

"I can't," he said tiredly. "I wasn't good enough for Chloe, but I ignored the signs for years and look where we ended up. I won't make that mistake again."

"I'm not like Chloe." If Emily knew anything for certain, it was that. She may be guilty of a multitude of sins, but she and Chloe were polar opposites. As different as gingerbread and French pastry.

"If you say so." He huffed. "Look, we jumped into this too quickly and got carried away. Neither of us have dated for a while, and it seemed like a good thing. But we need to take a step back. Get some distance."

He doesn't mean it, she told herself. *He's just emotional. We can talk when he calms down.*

"So, where do we stand?" she asked, insides quivering. "Are we still together?"

"No," he said, crushing her tender heart with one cold word. "I think it's best if we end things for now. Maybe we can reassess down the track."

Emily crumpled. She could hear the truth in his words. He didn't want her anymore, and knowing that ripped her apart inside as effectively as if he'd reached through the phone, torn her open and shredded her vital organs. She'd thought she was helping him, thought that they'd had something special, but instead she'd worsened his self-doubt and broken the bond they'd been building.

This mess was on her.

"Okay," she said. "I understand." She drew in a shuddering breath, tears streaming over her cheeks and dripping off her chin, dampening the knees of her jeans. "Do you want me to come by and collect the things I left there?"

The horrible things that had ruined their relationship, and the future she'd hoped they'd share. A pipe dream.

"No," he replied, after thinking for a moment. "I'll drop them off on your doorstep. It's easier that way."

Emily nodded, although she knew he couldn't see her. Then she hung up and curled into the fetal position, clutching herself, trying to take up as little space as she possible, wishing she could roll up so small that she just vanished. All she'd wanted was to make Justin happy, and instead she'd gone and broken her own heart. Stupid, stupid girl.

She'd cried.

Justin had done a lot of awful things in his time, but he'd never made a woman sob like the world was ending. He'd been hurt and trying to save them both future pain, but God, hearing her cry made him want to kick his own ass.

He was a shit. He deserved to be miserable.

No more women. They weren't worth it. He'd been okay on his own for the past year with Richie and Dan for company. He loved his family and had a few close friends he could go out for beers or watch rugby with. He enjoyed his job. He didn't need a woman.

But she'd cried.

Whatever her flaws, Emily obviously cared for him. Or at the very least, she'd cared about the idea of him. He shouldn't let her tears affect him like this. *He didn't care.* If he repeated that to himself often enough, he might believe it. But probably not.

With a curse, he tore the mountain wall hanging off and tossed it into the back of his truck. He grabbed the yellow cushions, then the painting. The cookie jar joined them. He didn't even stop to eat a cookie first. Then, the final touch, he piled the offensive pink mat and the toilet cover on top, slamming the door behind.

He looked around his living room. Job done. He'd exorcised Emily and all signs of her invasion. His home was exactly the way he liked it: plain, manly.

Boring.

THE DAY after Justin shut her out and returned everything she'd left at his house, Emily found herself sitting numbly behind the counter of her shop, speaking to Nina, a reporter from the local newspaper, the South Canterbury Chronicle.

She'd agreed to this interview weeks ago, when she'd been named South Canterbury Businesswoman of the Year, but now she'd rather be anywhere else. For the past twenty-four hours, she'd barely been able to string together two sentences without crying.

"So, Emily," Nina said, scribbling the date on the top of a notepad, "how long have you known you wanted to be a businesswoman?"

Emily gripped the sides of the stool she was sitting on and forced a smile. "To be honest, I don't think of myself as a businesswoman. I'm a florist and a decorator at heart, but I saw an opportunity to build something special for the community, so I went for it."

Nina tapped her pink and gold pen against her chin, watching Emily thoughtfully. She had intense eyes that were nearly black, and her outfit screamed 'career woman'. "Since you were named Businesswoman of the Year, a businesswoman is what you've become, regardless of what you set out to be. Speaking of the award, how do you feel about winning it?"

"Honored," Emily replied easily. "There were so many successful, hardworking women nominated that I never expected to win."

She wondered idly whether Nina would leave if she broke down in tears, or if that would only make her determined to discover the reason why. The journalist jotted some shorthand notes. How long did it take to master shorthand? Emily's friend Aria could write using shorthand as fast as most people could talk and Nina seemed equally adept. Maybe they had competed in timed drills at journalism school.

"Let's talk about the property you own and manage," Nina suggested.

"Do you mean the shop, or the old hotel?"

"The old hotel," Nina clarified. "Tell me what gave you the idea to restore it and rent it out to other businesses."

Emily's death grip on the stool eased. She could do this. When Nina had called requesting an interview, she'd nearly turned her down out of sheer nerves, but this was her life and her community. There were no wrong answers. And the publicity couldn't hurt.

"That building had been abandoned since I was a little girl and it always seemed like a real waste to me. I could see how much potential it had, and it's in a great location near the town center. When it came up for sale, I bought it impulsively. I wasn't sure exactly what to do with it, but I talked it through with my father—"

"Who sits on the town council?" Nina interrupted.

"That's correct. And Dad suggested that rather than reopening it as a hotel, I investigate other options. I asked around to see if anyone would be interested in renting a space there, and the response was overwhelming. Everyone wanted to support my project to see the old building restored, so I lined up future tenants and hired a team who specialize in restoring heritage buildings in a way that retains their original character. Some modifications were needed to make it suitable for commercial use, but I think they did a fantastic job."

"I agree," Nina said. "I visited before I came here. It's a lovely building. I've seen photos of how it looked beforehand, so I appreciate how much vision you must have had to see the potential in it."

Emily shrugged, uncomfortable with the praise. She had a talent for seeing how to make the best of things, that was all.

Nina referred back to her list of questions. "So, the building is fully occupied now?"

"Yes, it is." And thank God for that. Emily had sunk her finances into the building, so it was a relief to see her sacrifice and hard work pay off. That the community loved it only made her happier.

"I spoke to some of your tenants while I was there," Nina said. "They had a lot of good things to say about you. Couldn't stop them as a matter of fact." Her lips quirked up. "So tell me about the shop. How long have you had it?"

"I opened four years ago, after I completed a certificate in floral design and a diploma in retail management at the poly-technic."

"And things are going well?"

"They are," Emily confirmed. "I love it. Business is relatively steady, with some fluctuation between summer and winter tourist seasons, and there's really nowhere I'd rather be."

Except at this very minute, she'd rather be at home in bed, hidden beneath the covers.

"That's great to hear." Nina didn't look up. "So many women settle for positions which don't truly make them happy or fulfill their potential because society tells them they can't have it all. It always makes me happy to see a woman living the life she wants."

Emily blushed. She wanted to dismiss the compliment out of hand, but the truth was, she did have it good. She *should* be proud.

"Thank you," she said simply.

"No." Nina met her eyes, deadly serious. "Thank *you*. You're serving as a great role model for local girls."

Now, Emily's gaze did slide away, and she murmured, "I don't know about that."

A great role model wouldn't have let her dream guy go without a fight.

"I do. So, in saying that, is there any advice you have for girls or women out there who aspire to be a businesswoman?"

"Go for it. If you work hard enough and believe in yourself, nothing can stop you."

"That's great. Well said." Nina tucked her notepad into the Prada handbag she'd deposited on the counter, gathered her dark hair into a bun and stabbed the fancy pen through it. "Thank you for agreeing to speak with me," she said, reaching over to shake Emily's hand. Then she straightened her tailored pantsuit and slung the handbag over her shoulder. "It was a pleasure to meet you. Good luck for the year ahead."

"You, too," Emily said, waving her off.

Once the frighteningly intense journalist had left, Emily's shoulders slumped, and she drew in a shaky breath. The interview had gone well as far as she could tell. She could finally go home, build a pillow fort, and hide from the world. At least for a night.

wo mornings after Justin reclaimed his home, he found himself opening the curtains and windows to let the sun in. The day before, he'd kept them shut, just because he could, but it had been gloomy and, above all else, pointless. Nobody noticed except for him, and he had nothing to prove to himself. So, he reasoned, there was no harm in letting the sunshine and fresh air into the house.

As he ate a bowl of chocolate-flavored cereal with full-fat milk and a glass of fruit juice, the same breakfast he'd had for the past year, because no one was around to force him to eat organic quinoa puffs with goji berries and almond milk, he looked around his living area, really paying attention for once. He'd lived here for a while, but no one would know it. Whether out of sheer stubbornness—because with Chloe he'd always had to have the perfect piece of art on the wall, or the most fashionable style of furniture—or perhaps simple laziness, he'd never taken the time to make this house his own after the breakup.

He'd been determined not to live as he had with Chloe, afraid to get comfortable in his own home, but he may have gone too far in the other direction and shot himself in the foot.

It just so happened that he liked art—some art, anyway—and a little color wasn't so bad. Maybe he could occupy a middle ground, where he didn't go back to the way he'd lived with Chloe, but didn't keep a militarily bland home, either.

So, he made a trip into the nearby city of Timaru that evening after work to purchase a plush new rug for the living room and a canvas photo of a forested waterfall to hang next to the TV. Something small enough that it wouldn't detract focus from sports games when they were on. As he laid the rug on the floor and hung the photo, he felt like he was recovering a little bit of himself. And he liked it.

"I'M SO *STUPID*."

Emily sat cross-legged on her bed, stuffed another chocolate in her mouth and chewed, barely tasting it. Her friend, Kayla, the chocolatier, winced at her blasphemous treatment of the high-end treat, but Emily didn't care. Picking another chocolate from the tray, she bit into it and some kind of alcoholic filling oozed from the center.

"He could have been *The One*," she continued. "And I went and ruined it by coming on too strong, then having no spine to back myself up." She hiccupped through a sob, then blew her nose vigorously. Kayla, bless her heart, said nothing. "I could have fixed everything if I'd explained myself properly or talked to him earlier rather than just giving into my impulses, but you know what I'm like."

Kayla nodded, and Emily sighed. Of course she did. *Everyone* knew what Emily was like. The minute anyone said an angry word, she became a blubbering mess.

"You're sweet, Em," Kayla said. "I'm sure you meant well. He shouldn't have talked to you like that. What an asshole."

"He's not an asshole," Emily said, defending him. "He's a sensitive man, and I hurt him when all I wanted was to make him happy. I didn't want to change him. He's like Goldilocks' porridge—just right."

"You read too many fairytales, sweetie."

She knew she did. Perhaps that was the problem. She'd always hoped if she believed hard enough and did enough good in the world then she'd get the happy ending she wanted.

She buried her face in a pillow and screamed. Kayla's soft touch landed on the back of her head, stroking her hair, and she soaked in the comfort her friend offered, the physical contact like a balm for her soul. She was a toucher. It made her feel connected. Valued. *Loved.*

Lifting her face from the pillow, she twisted and embraced Kayla. "Thanks, girl."

"No problem. I'll be here any time you want to shit-talk a man. Or not shit-talk him, as the case may be. But gosh, I wish I could tell Justin you think he's sensitive. Could you imagine the look on his face?" She giggled. "Can I tell him? Pretty please?"

Kayla's teasing had the desired effect, bringing Emily out of her melancholy for a moment.

"No!" she shrieked, laughing through her tears. "Don't you dare!" Then she remembered the way she'd fallen short at the first hurdle. "I'm so weeeeak," she moaned. "I need to be better."

"You are who you are, Em. Not much you can do about that."

"I can be better," Emily said firmly. Or if she couldn't, she'd have to resort to dating men who never argued with her. Frankly, she didn't think she'd find one of those rare creatures, and if she did, he'd bore her senseless. No, she needed to do better, and she needed to do it *now*. Justin deserved a full explanation. She didn't want to reinforce his negative view of either her gender or himself.

"I know you can, Em." Kayla laid her head in Emily's lap. "But you should know you're perfect as you are.

Emily scoffed at the idea of that. Wouldn't it be nice? But no one was perfect. Not Chloe, not Justin, and certainly not her.

～

"Hey, bro. How goes it?" Cooper breezed in Justin's front door with a friendly grin.

"Just peachy," Justin replied, wondering why his brother was always so damned perky. Must be a side effect of frequent sex with beautiful women. Justin wouldn't know; he wasn't getting any.

"Oooh." Cooper winced and slapped him on the back. "That bad?"

"I said, everything is fine," Justin snapped.

"Dude, that's what women say when everything is the opposite of fine. How was the date with Emily?" he asked, immediately zeroing in on the problem.

"Good." Too good to be true. He should have taken that as a warning.

"Good?" Cooper smirked as he flopped onto the couch beside Justin and put his feet on the coffee table. He glanced down. "Nice mat, is it new?"

"Yeah."

Cooper nodded and didn't seem to think anything of it. "The date was good. That's all you've got to say?"

"Damn good," Justin admitted. "But it didn't work out."

"Why the hell not? You know she's so far out of your league, it's like she's in a whole other ball game."

"Yeah I know that," Justin said, impatience evident in his tone. "And so does she, apparently. Didn't waste any time trying to change me."

He expected Cooper to be appalled on his behalf. Perhaps commiserate about fickle women. But instead, Cooper crossed his arms and eyed Justin as if *he* were the bad guy.

"Are we talking about the same Emily? The nicest person in

Itirangi? The town's favorite darling? Never has a bad word to say about anyone? *That* Emily?"

Justin didn't like his implication. "You think I misunderstood."

"I *know* you did. You're my brother and I love you, but you can be thick-skulled. If Emily was willing to put up with you, that pretty much qualifies her for sainthood, in my opinion." Cooper shook his head in disgust. "And you pushed her away."

"She put a fluffy pink abomination in my bathroom," Justin grumbled, disgruntled by the attack on his character. "She's the one who messed up here."

Cooper's eyes lit up and he whooped with laughter. "Shit, man. That's priceless."

Justin's lip curled in annoyance. "I'm not a fluffy pink kind of guy."

"Based on that, you thought she was trying to change you?" Cooper asked, getting hold of himself. "Not every woman is Chloe, buddy. She made a mistake. From what I've seen, Emily hardly ever dates. She miscalculated. She's not perfect."

Perhaps not, but for a few days, Justin had thought she was.

He considered this fresh perspective. Emily was human. Humans made mistakes. But after what he'd been through with Chloe and the years he'd wasted, the idea of taking a risk on Emily and hoping she was different... Well, it was terrifying.

"Do you still have the fluffy pink thing?" Cooper asked.

Justin didn't dignify the question with an answer.

THE BLANK PIECE of paper taunted Emily. Laughed up at her with its whiteness. Half an hour ago she'd chosen the most masculine, no-frills stationery in her shop and set about writing a letter to Justin. Here she was, with a headache and nothing to show for it.

Pursing her lips, she wrote in flowing cursive across the top, *Dear Justin.*

There, she'd made a start. Now she just needed to fill in the rest of the blank space. Perhaps sending a letter was wimpy, but she knew she'd have a meltdown if she tried to speak to him face-to-face or over the phone. She wasn't equipped for verbal confrontation. Text messaging seemed too blasé, and an email, too cold. Which left good, old-fashioned letter writing.

While she didn't care about defending herself, she couldn't let Justin continue to believe anything was wrong with him, or that he hadn't been good enough. That was flat-out not true. Taking a deep breath, she shored up her courage. She could do this. In fact, she had an entire uninterrupted evening to get her thoughts down on paper now that the shop had closed, and she'd locked the door. She added another sentence. *Please hear me out.* Good, she was making progress. *I'd like to explain why I brought those things over to your house. I can't stand knowing that you think I wanted to change you.* God, even committing these words to paper made her stomach turn. She swallowed, ignoring the nausea. Her fear of confrontation could be debilitating at times.

Nibbling on her lower lip, searching for the right words, she started a new paragraph. *For as long as I can remember, I've wanted to make people happy, and one of the best ways I've found to do that is to surround them with things that please them. Pretty pictures, happy colors. I always thought I was good at matching people with the things that complemented them.* Although he had her questioning that.

"Don't," she told herself sternly. "Don't lose confidence in yourself. You made one mistake, that's all."

Okay, maybe a couple of mistakes. But the pink mat and toilet cover had been the last straw, and to be honest, she couldn't even remember why she'd thought it was a good idea. She suspected she'd been thinking of herself rather than Justin. Imagining herself in that bathroom when he invited her to live with him. But she'd gotten ahead of herself. Way ahead. She should have kept it simple, with things she knew he would like, or not encroached at all.

I've made a career of it, she added. *All I wanted to do was brighten up your place, to make you happy. I wasn't trying to change you. I wouldn't want you to change.* Her hand shook as she wrote, smudging the ink in places and ruining her beautiful handwriting. She stared at the last full stop. Now all that was left was to put everything on the line, to go big or go home. Did she have the courage to put herself out there, knowing she'd probably be disappointed?

This is Justin, she reminded herself. *He's worth it.* If nothing else, she wanted him to understand how highly she thought of him. How much he meant to her.

There's a good chance I'm falling in love with you, she wrote. *I don't care what your house looks like. If you want to live in a dungeon, that's fine with me, as long as you're happy. Of course, I can't guarantee I'd want to live in the dungeon with you... But we could work out the particulars later.*

She was really doing this. Putting her innermost thoughts and feelings in ink. Writing them down made them feel more legitimate. Irrevocable. She plowed onward. *If you still want nothing to do with me, I understand. I didn't write this letter looking for forgiveness. I wrote it as a friend who wanted you to know the truth.* Signing her name at the bottom, she folded the paper and slipped it into an envelope, then sealed it before she could rethink her choice of words.

Then she locked it in the top drawer of her desk.

On Saturday evening, Justin visited his sister, as he usually did. Since she'd returned to Itirangi a year ago, friends and family had been invited to dinner at Aria's house every Saturday. Her return to town had happened to coincide with Justin's unceremonious dumping by Chloe, and attending the weekly get-together allowed him to pretend he had a social life. Plus, it got him out of his house. He tired of his own company, and when that happened, Dan and Ritchie tired of him. They showed it in nasty ways, predominantly with their claws.

He arrived fifteen minutes late, like always, the better to ensure he was never alone with his nosy sister—whom he adored, mind you—and also never had the dubious honor of being the last to show up. No one wanted to be the guy who delayed dinner.

"Hi, Justin," Aria said, hugging him when he strode through the doorway.

He hugged her back, then held her by the shoulders to examine her. "Hey, Ri," he replied. "You're, uh, eye-catching today."

Seeing her in a lime-green tank top and electric-blue

leggings, it was the kindest comment he could think of. His sister was, by his estimation, the most memorable woman in Itirangi. Her eclectic taste, which often ran to vivid, clashing colors and quirky jewelry, and her no-holds-barred approach to friendship tended to startle people. But they adjusted quickly, because Aria also had a big heart and the best of intentions.

"I try," she said with a smile. "Take a seat. Mum and Dad are already here."

"Do you need a hand with the cooking?"

She shook her head. "Thanks, I've got it under control. You can get some plates and cutlery out, if you want."

He began to do what he was told, but then Aria grabbed his arm and frowned up at him.

"Are you okay? You seem a little…off."

"Off, how?"

She shrugged. "I don't know. But there may as well be a black rain cloud hanging over your head. You look pretty grim."

He blinked, astonished anyone could distinguish his mood today from his mood every other day. Either it was a testament to Aria's superior power of observation, or a sign of how truly wretched he looked.

"Mind your own business. I'm fine."

Even as he said it, he cringed internally. He sounded like a pouty teenager, and Aria didn't seem to believe him in the slightest. But after raising a doubtful brow, she turned away and resumed cooking. He sniffed, trying to figure out what was in the pot, and his mouth watered. Mmm. Some kind of curry. Probably vegetarian, since Aria didn't eat meat, but curry was curry; he wasn't fussy. He found a stack of plates, piled cutlery on top, and carried them to the dinner table, situated near a wall in the kitchen. Aria liked to keep the table in the kitchen so that she could be amongst her family while she cooked. The kitchen was the heart of her home.

"Hey, Mum, Dad," Justin said, dragging a chair over to join his parents, Donna and Geoff, who were sipping mugs of tea.

His mum gave him a look. "Is that any way to greet your mother? Get over here and give me a hug."

Justin exchanged a long-suffering look with his dad. She had her kids wrapped around her finger and she knew it. A short, slightly rounded woman, Donna gave warm, motherly hugs. Once Justin had squeezed her, he sat down.

A knock sounded on the door, then Cooper strolled in, claimed a seat beside Justin, and said, "Are you still moping?"

"Aha!" In a flash, Aria was next to them. "I knew something was wrong," she declared.

"Well, obviously," Cooper agreed. "Just look at his grumpy face. He's even more miserable than usual."

"What's the matter, honey?" his mum asked, concerned.

He had the worst siblings ever. Never had the world seen a more obnoxious pair. He glowered and silently condemned them to the deepest pits of hell. "Nothing is wrong," he bit out. "Everything is great."

"He's having trouble in his love life," Cooper said, speaking from behind a hand as though sharing a secret. And he was, damn it, but it wasn't his secret to share.

Justin groaned and looked at the ceiling. "Why do I ever tell you anything?"

Aria glanced between them. "I thought your love life was nonexistent. What am I missing?"

"Nothing," Justin grunted, at the same time as Cooper said, "He's hung up on Emily Parker."

"Emily?" Aria beamed, apparently delighted. "Good choice. I'd love to have her as my sister. How long have you been dating?"

Justin picked at a callus on his palm and wondered whether he could get away with stonewalling her. If Aria knew what had happened with Emily, it wouldn't be long before her friends knew, and from there the gossip could spiral wildly out of control. He knew how quickly the grapevine worked in Itirangi. Not to mention, Aria would probably side with Emily.

Cooper took the choice away. "They aren't dating," he told her, shaking his head sadly. "Anymore, that is. Emily moved a few things into his house, and he had a meltdown and broke it off."

The temperature in the room dropped ten degrees as all of his family members, bar none, pinned him with chilly stares. He shifted, uncomfortable under the weight of their combined disapproval.

Aria cleared her throat. "Let me get this right. So, Emily—who's the sweetest person ever and completely gorgeous and whom every single guy in Itirangi has asked out at least once—agreed to date you, and then *you* rejected *her* because she was trying to make a place for herself in your life?"

"I didn't reject her," Justin muttered. "She rejected me. She was trying to change me."

"Did you ask her why she did what she did?" Geoff asked. Avoiding his wife's gaze, he added, "Women's motivations are often not what we think they are. Sometimes, the things they do make sense to them, but not to us."

"Have you been reading self-help books?" Cooper queried with a grin.

Geoff shrugged. "Your mother leaves them in the bathroom. Gotta read something when you're on the loo."

Justin scowled, preferring not to picture his father reading *Men Are from Mars, Women Are from Venus'* while taking a crap.

"I didn't ask," he replied. "It was perfectly obvious."

"I thought I raised you better," Donna said, sounding disappointed.

Justin hunched his shoulders and ducked his head. He *hated* when his mum sounded disappointed, preferring her to just knock him over the head with a hard-covered book and get on with it.

"You shouldn't assume the worst without getting all of the

facts," she continued. "I know Chloe broke your heart, but not all women are the same."

Justin flinched at the reminder of his failed relationship. But for once, rather than hurting when he heard Chloe's name, he felt nothing other than embarrassment that anyone could still think he cared for her.

"You should give Emily the benefit of the doubt," Aria insisted. "Or at least give her the opportunity to defend herself."

The thing was, *he had*. When he'd called her that morning, she could have explained why she'd brought those things around, but when she apologized, that seemed as good as an admission of guilt. If he'd been wrong, she would have told him to pull his head out of his ass. Wouldn't she have?

If the roles were reversed, he certainly would have told her to in no uncertain terms. He would have yelled until she heard his point of view. But Emily wasn't like him. In all the years he'd known her, he couldn't ever recall her raising her voice, let alone arguing with anyone. Every person she met adored her, and because of that, he'd assumed it was in her nature to be easygoing, but perhaps, for whatever reason, she was incapable of telling people when she thought they were being a jerk. Perhaps he shouldn't have assumed her guilt simply because she hadn't reacted as he would have in that situation.

He felt a twinge of guilt. He'd said things that would have been hard for anyone to hear, but especially someone as soft as Emily.

What if he'd made a mistake?

EMILY WOKE STUPIDLY EARLY on Monday and drove to the shop. She unlocked the door, then the top drawer of her desk, in order to retrieve the letter for Justin. She'd given the manner and time of delivery a great deal of thought and decided the best option was a weekday morning, before he woke, so she didn't risk running into him while she dropped the letter off. If he came outside while she was sticking it in the mailbox, she thought she'd die from mortification, but she had no problem creeping around like a wuss.

Returning to her car, she drove to Justin's house and parked a few hundred yards away, so the sound of the engine wouldn't wake him up. She left the car idling, walked the distance to the mailbox, slid the envelope inside, and dashed back to the car, slamming it into gear and taking off as quickly as possible. Her heart galloped madly, and her breath came in puffs, whether from the running or anxiety, she didn't know. By the time she arrived back at the shop, nervous sweat had plastered her shirt to her back. Resting her forehead on the steering wheel, she calmed her breathing and waited for the sweat to dry before going inside to start her workday.

WHEN JUSTIN DROVE past his mailbox on the way to check the pest traps on Monday morning, he noticed an envelope protruding from the slit and hit the brakes. Since the envelope hadn't been there yesterday, and it was too early in the morning for the postman to have come by, someone must have hand-delivered it either late last night or early this morning.

Feeling apprehensive, he wound down the window and snatched the envelope from the slot. It had no postal stamp, which meant his deduction about it being hand-delivered was correct. His name was written on the front in an elegant, looping handwriting he didn't recognize, and when he ripped the envelope open, he withdrew a handwritten letter in that same looping script.

Who could it possibly be from? He hadn't received a hand-written letter since Cooper had been stationed overseas with the Navy a few years ago.

He scanned the words and his blood ran cold. Then he re-read it to make sure it really said what he thought it said and laid it down. Closing his eyes, his hands fisted on his thighs. *Shit.* He'd screwed up epically. Just as his family had suspected, sweet lovable Emily had only been trying to make him happy. Maybe she'd mis-stepped, but she'd had good intentions. And he'd lumped her in with Chloe because of it.

If only she'd said something at the time.

No, I shouldn't have leapt to conclusions. God, he'd been a total bastard. The things he'd said to her.

He was unworthy of her, and he'd proved it that day. Yet here she was, writing him a goddamn letter just so he didn't feel bad about himself. Well, he felt pretty fucking awful right now.

His gut twisted itself painfully into knots. Perhaps he could go to her and apologize. Tell her that he appreciated everything she'd tried to do and that he'd be happy for her to decorate in future, provided she consulted him first. In fact, he couldn't imagine anything he'd like more than to choose new decor *with* Emily, for a home they'd share. He skimmed over the letter again, reading each sentence individually, searching for any sign she still cared for him.

There's a good chance I'm falling in love with you, she'd written. He focused on that lone sentence, which filled him with hope. But despair quickly followed. He didn't deserve Emily. Even if she gave him another chance, he'd do something stupid to screw it up. He didn't know how to be the guy who did right by her. Chloe had messed him up ten different ways and left him unable to engage in a normal relationship.

He *could* go to Emily and spill his guts, tell her how crazy he was about her and how he was sorry for treating her the way he had. Knowing what a sweetheart she was, she'd probably forgive him. And for a while, it would be bliss. But what was to stop him from hurting her in future? She was delicate, emotionally if not physically. He...wasn't. Remembering the sounds of her sobs over the phone, he didn't think he could stand to hurt her again.

So, what would he do?

For now, nothing. He needed time to think, to un-muddle his head. A day, maybe two. Then he'd decide what came next. He had time. The most important thing was that he do this right.

11

The day after Emily delivered the letter to Justin, her morning had started poorly and gotten worse. Upon waking, she'd rolled over, blinked bleary eyes and checked her phone for messages from Justin. No new voicemails, no new texts, which meant the letter she'd written hadn't affected him at all.

No, don't think like that. She needed to remember that the aim of writing the letter hadn't been to win him back—although she couldn't deny she'd hoped that would be the end result—but rather to make sure he knew she thought he was perfect as he was. And now he did.

She'd just have to be satisfied with that.

Compared to the past few weeks, the shop was quiet. Peaceful. The buzz of Christmas, Boxing Day and New Year's had finished, and locals had returned to work. Tourists still lingered in the area, and she had a steady stream of customers to keep her busy, but she found herself missing the frantic rush that had occupied her mind so she didn't have time to dwell on her bittersweet New Year's romance. Now, in between exchanging pleasantries and ringing up items, her mind wandered to those days and nights with Justin when she'd been wonderfully, recklessly happy.

Then, late in the afternoon, her mood plunged dramatically. A teenage girl with bleached blonde hair and dark eyeliner entered the shop and slowly circuited it, picking products up, then placing them back on the shelf. She seemed bored, like she was killing time.

Emily watched her, refraining from offering help because the way the girl hunched her shoulders and averted her eyes said she wanted to be left alone. But something about the girl's furtive attitude unsettled her, so rather than preparing bouquets as she usually would during the downtime, she stayed at the counter and started tallying sales. When it happened, the girl moved so quickly Emily wondered if she'd imagined it, but then the girl shifted, and the outline of the daisy wreath she'd slipped down her shirt protruded through the fabric, giving her away.

A shoplifter. Emily's gut churned. It wasn't unheard of for tourists to try their luck at Pretty Things, but usually they only dared during busy times when she and Sandra were distracted. She'd never seen anyone so blatant. Keeping her expression neutral, Emily reached for her phone and selected Sergeant Gareth Wayland's mobile number. Hands shaking, she typed out a message, earmarked 'URGENT'.

Shoplifter in my store. Please come help.

She didn't do anything else, waiting until she received a reply.

Two minutes away. Don't let them leave.

What did one say or do to prevent a thief from leaving their shop? Emily wasn't prepared to physically stop her. The daisy wreath wasn't worth it. If it came to that, she'd simply let the girl go and issue a trespass order if she tried to return.

Taking a deep breath, she plastered a phony smile on her face. "Nice day out there, isn't it?"

The girl mumbled something.

"Pardon?" Emily said. "I couldn't hear you."

"It'd be better if I wasn't here," the girl snarled, louder.

Emily flinched, taken aback by the naked hostility in her glare. "Are you here with your family?" she asked, searching for a way to continue the conversation before the girl stalked out. "Stuck until they're ready to go home?"

The girl's chin jerked. "Something like that. But the trip has no end date. I could be here for a day, or a month." She scowled darkly. "I won't last a month in this hellhole."

Emily blinked rapidly. "I beg your pardon?"

The girl's lips firmed in a sullen line. "You heard me."

At that moment, the door swung open and Sergeant Gareth Wayland strode inside. Tall and broad, with a stiff bearing and a square jaw, Gareth could intimidate most people into confessing with nothing more than a look. Fortunately for Emily, she'd never been on the receiving end of that frightening expression. He folded his arms over his uniformed chest, jaw working as he chewed gum, and leveled his famous glare at the temperamental shoplifter.

"You have some explaining to do, young lady."

Then the door opened a second time to admit Aria Simons. Fantastic. Another reason to add today to her official list of the worst days ever. Aria may be lovely, but she was also naturally inquisitive, and—an added bonus—a reminder of the man Emily was trying to forget.

Aria stopped just inside the door. "What's going on?" she asked. "Gareth?"

Emily squeezed her hands into fists and prayed for the whole godforsaken day to end.

Justin was nursing a pint of beer at Davy's Bar when Gareth pulled up a stool to join him.

"I'll have what he's having," Gareth said to Davy, the Irishman who owned the establishment.

Davy poured another pint and slid it across to Gareth. "You look wrecked," he told the sergeant. "What was it today? Rescuing Mrs. Dodd's mangy cat from another tree? Busting a cheating ring at the high school?"

Justin chuckled. On many occasions, he'd seen Gareth up a tree, frail Mrs. Dodds waiting below, and he never failed to snap a photo. Never knew when that might come in handy.

"Shoplifting teenager at Pretty Things," Gareth replied. "You know how Em is. She was shaken up."

Justin snapped to attention and his knee whacked the underside of the bar, throbbing painfully. "There was a shoplifter at Emily's place? Is she okay?" Tension rocketed through his body as images flooded his mind. Emily, terrified as some hoodlum threatened her, or hugging her knees and crying once the thug left, then going home and feeling unsafe in her own bed.

She hadn't called him.

Fear gripped his stomach. He would never even have known if not for Gareth. Emily hadn't turned to him for comfort, or to chase down the little shit and make them sorry. Justin itched to smash something. He thumped his fist on the bar, the impact sending jarring shock waves up to his elbow.

"Calm the hell down," Gareth rumbled. "Emily is fine. She didn't even need me in the end. Your sister turned up and sorted everything out. Bit disappointing, actually. I was looking forward to playing the hero."

Justin growled. He *actually* growled. Like one of the wild animals he encountered in his line of work. Emily didn't *need* the sergeant to be a hero for her. *Justin* would be her hero. Every other man could go to the devil.

"Was that you?" Davy asked, bemused. "I gotta say, I'm worried, man. I know you don't get out much, but growling isn't generally how we communicate around here."

Ignoring him, Justin considered what Gareth had said: Aria had come to the rescue. His emotions jumbled together until he couldn't recognize one from another. He was grateful to Aria for being there, but oddly envious. *It should have been him.*

But it never would be him, he realized. As long as he stayed away from Emily, hesitating and dithering like his sister in a shoe shop, she'd never come to him for support or ask him to be her rock, no matter how badly he wanted her to. What's more, he had no right to expect anything different. He wasn't entitled to know what was going on in her life any more than Gareth or Davy, and that simply wasn't good enough.

Forget about taking time out to think, he needed to go after what he really wanted.

Sinking into a hot bath, Emily felt the troubles of the day ease away. Warm water embraced her body and soothed the tension from her shoulders. Then someone knocked on her front door. Lowering her ears beneath the water, she ignored them. Whoever it was, they were only going to make her crappy day crappier, and she deserved a break from reality. She closed her eyes and tensed then released the muscles in each limb, one by one, working her way from her shoulders down to her toes.

Vaguely, she became aware of a thundering noise, closer than the front door; someone was in her house. She straightened, water sluicing down her back. If she lived anywhere other than Itirangi, she might be concerned by the sound of a person in her house, but most likely it was just a friend who didn't want to wait outside. She never locked the door, so anyone could walk on in. She wrung her hair out and wrapped a towel around her body. As she did so, the bathroom door flew open and Justin filled the doorway, broad shoulders heaving, staring at her with some unfamiliar emotion glowing in his eyes.

Well, *that* was unexpected.

She clasped the towel tightly to her chest, pulse spiking so high she feared she might faint.

"What are you doing?" she demanded. "You frightened me out of my wits."

Justin's mouth fell open. Then he snapped it shut, his throat working as he swallowed. "You—"

"Are nearly naked," Emily finished for him. "This is *my* bathroom. In *my* house. Which I didn't invite you into."

He glowered, and she wished she didn't notice how handsome he looked, his swarthy complexion improved by the flush on his cheeks, his hair recently cut but mussed, his beard tidy. Clearly, he hadn't gone to pieces after their breakup.

"Are you just going to stand there?" she asked. Her nerve, a by-product of fear and indignation, began to wane. "Why are you here?"

She'd delivered the letter first thing yesterday. It wasn't as if he could have just discovered it and rushed over here, although he certainly looked like he'd rushed from somewhere. When he didn't reply, she stepped out of the bath, onto the mat. Her movement seemed to jolt him into action. He hurried forward, arms open, and embraced her tightly.

"Justin, I'm all wet," she protested, but couldn't push him away without dropping the towel. Not that modesty mattered at this point, but the towel felt like a protective layer between them.

"I don't care," he growled into her hair. "Let me hold you."

His strong biceps bulged where they banded around her upper arms. She could feel his warmth through the damp fabric of his shirt, and his heart pounded frantically beneath her ear.

"Please don't hold me like this when you don't love me," she muttered, desperate to put some distance between them so she wouldn't turn to mush because of the way he held her as though she were vital to him.

"I can't let you go," he said helplessly, as though he didn't fully understand it himself. "Not now, not ever."

Her heart leapt into her throat. Did he mean that? She wanted to believe, but she was afraid to. "What are you saying? What's going on, Justin?"

"You're mine," he said, his large body trembling as he spoke. "But you didn't come to me. Something bad happened to you, and you didn't tell me about it. Didn't let me fix it for you."

Something in her deflated. So, that's what this was about. He didn't miss her, he was just annoyed he hadn't had the opportunity to save the day.

"It wasn't a big deal," she told him. And maybe, to another woman, that might have been true, but to her, it was yet another symptom of how terribly this year was going when they were barely even two weeks into it. For the sake of her dignity, she forced herself to say, "No need to look so torn up about it. I'm fine. You checked on me. Now you can go."

"Don't lie to me, Em." He leaned back, tilted her chin up, and searched her gaze. "I know you better than that."

"No." Emily shoved his chest, towel be damned, but he held firm. "You don't get to act like you care about me," she hissed, forgetting the fact she didn't like conflict. Self-preservation instincts had kicked in and she forgot anything except the way she'd hurt when he dropped her like she didn't matter. "Please don't pretend you care." A tear trickled down her cheek and dripped onto his shirt. "If you wanted me in your life, you would have said something by now. You can't do this to me, it's not fair."

Justin resisted her attempts to throw him off. "I know it's not fair," he said softly. "But I do care about you, Em. So, so much. I wanted to take the time to think everything through, to make sure we did it right this time around. You deserve that. But then it scared the hell out of me when Gareth said what happened. I was so worried about you. And do you know how much it hurt to realize that if not for Gareth, I wouldn't have known anything was wrong? Worse, that I had no *right* to know?"

"Just like I had no right to call you," she said, meeting his eyes, refusing to give into the impulse to look away. "You're not my boyfriend, and I vividly remember you saying we should keep it that way in future."

He groaned. "I was wrong, sweetheart. I made assumptions and let my fear get the better of me and I'm sorry for that." He nuzzled her forehead, pressing soft kisses along her hairline. "I screwed up badly. I know that. But I'm falling in love with you, Emily Parker, and I hope you'll let me prove it."

"You are?" Emily prided herself on not stuttering. Her insides had turned to warm goo. "But I wrote you that letter and you ignored it."

"Like I said, I was thinking. But that was stupid. I should have come to you straight away." He drew back, meeting her eyes so she could read his sincerity. "I was an ass. I should have given you the benefit of the doubt. I'm sorry."

Emily nibbled her lip. Could this really be happening? Was Justin actually here, in her bathroom, confessing his love for her? Or, at least, something a lot like love. It was a high school fantasy come true. But it was even better than the fantasy, because this was real. Justin was flesh and blood, a man who made mistakes, but who was falling for her the same way she was for him.

"I'm sorry for getting carried away," she said.

"The pink fluffy toilet cover was a bit hard to stomach," he said, smoothing a hand down the side of her face. "But I completely overreacted and blew it out of proportion. The fact of the matter is, you're too good for me, Em—nobody's been shy about making sure I know that—but I want another chance anyway. I want to be the person you turn to when you need help. I want to have the right to be annoyed if I hear things about you from another man. Please, say you'll give me that chance."

She cocked her head and studied him, as if taking the time to consider her options. A muscle in his jaw twitched. She smiled, then cupped his face between her palms and kissed him. There was nothing to think about. She was crazy for him. Maybe that made her just plain crazy, but so be it.

"Of course, I will. But next time you're upset, talk to me about it before you get to the point of no return."

"Promise." He kissed her back, completely serious and uncharacteristically tender. "Do you promise to bear with me even though I'm bound to mess up another ten thousand times or so?"

"I promise," she vowed. "As long as you give me your all."

"I will." His lips lifted in a sexy grin. "Now, can I peel that towel off your glorious body and make love to you?"

"Want to join me in the bath? It's still warm."

He glanced at it. "I'll never fit."

She giggled. "I trust you to be creative."

With a deep groan, he claimed her lips, thrusting his tongue between them. She gasped at the sensual invasion, then as quickly as the kiss started, it ended.

"How about the bedroom?" he rumbled.

She watched him from beneath heavy eyelids, pouting mischievously. "That's no fun."

"You won't be saying that soon."

He bent and tossed her over his shoulder. She squealed and swatted his backside but didn't fight too hard. After all, she kind of liked it when he manhandled her.

"Okay, okay," she laughed. "You can make love to me in the bed."

"Good." He made for the bedroom, with her hanging over his shoulder. "I'm crazy for you, Emily, and I'm going to make sure you know it."

He stepped through the doorway and turned around, then allowed her to slide down the front of his body.

"Be my girlfriend?" he asked.

She rolled her eyes. "What is this, high school?"

His mouth curled into a smirk. "Well, you have had a crush on me since then, remember?"

"I may have had a crush on that boy," she said coyly, "but I'm head over heels about the man he became."

"I'll never deserve you," he murmured, "but I'm going to do my damnedest to make sure you never regret being with me."

"I won't," she swore. "I love your family, your cats. I'm not totally sold on your house, but it has good bones and a great location. We can work with it. More importantly, you're my One."

He chuckled. "And you're mine."

She pressed a finger to his lips. "Shh. Stop talking and put your money where your mouth is."

He looked at her with wonder, as if she was the answer to all of the world's greatest riddles.

"How did I ever live without you?"

"Unhappily," she suggested.

Now it was his turn to cover her mouth. With his lips. And he didn't stop for a long, long time.

NEW YEAR'S EVE, LATER THAT YEAR

Emily burrowed beneath the thin blanket on the love-seat outside their house. A fire roared in the brazier and she poked a marshmallow into the flames, watching as it browned, then pulled it out and waited until it was cool enough to eat. The delicious sugary insides melted in her mouth.

"Yum."

"You gonna share with me?" Justin asked, unable to toast one for himself since he'd been trapped by Dan and Ritchie, who were curled together on his lap like a yin-yang symbol.

"Of course."

Emily grabbed another marshmallow from the packet and jabbed the skewer through it, holding it over the heat. Justin liked his marshmallows blacker than she did, so she waited for it to catch fire then blew it out. Taking the sticky blob between her fingers, she fed it to him. His mouth closed over her fingers, licking the sugar from her skin. She hummed contentedly.

"Can you do me another favor?" he asked.

He looked so adorable, not wanting to disturb his two fluffy emotional terrorists, that she'd agree to almost anything. "Sure thing."

"Reach into the pocket of my jeans."

She raised an eyebrow. "If this is some weird sexual game—"

"It's not," he said. "Please."

"Okay." She reached into the pocket, her touch landing on a smooth box. A box exactly the right size to hold a ring. Surely not. She gaped, her brain short-circuiting. "Is that what I think it is?"

"Why don't you pull it out and see?"

With clumsy fingers, she extracted the box and flipped the lid to reveal a gold ring with three identical diamonds set into the center of the band. "Wow," she breathed. "It's beautiful."

"The diamonds represent our past, present, and future," he explained, as she lifted it carefully from the box and slid it onto her finger. "A year ago today, I first kissed you. I thought it was fitting that we start next year with my ring on your finger. I love you Emily, and I want to be your future."

"Yes," she squeaked, ogling the ring and the way it glimmered in the light.

But the glimmer of the ring was nothing compared to the way Justin's eyes sparkled when he smiled at her. "I haven't even asked the question yet."

"Sorry," she said, meeting his eyes and waiting patiently. "Was there something you wanted to ask me, darling?"

His lips twitched. "Will you marry me?"

"Yes," she repeated, lifting the blanket and dumping the cats unceremoniously on the ground. For once, she wasn't going to share her man with them. "I love you," she told him. "I want to be your future, too, bringing brightness into your life forever."

Then she kissed her future husband, the love of her life, the gruff man with a heart of gold.

And she knew she'd never stop loving him.

"I have news for you, too," she said, ready to drop a bombshell of her own. "How do you feel about being a dad?"

"Are you kidding?" he asked.

She shook her head. "Serious as can be."

His hand went automatically to her stomach. "Are you sure?"

She nodded. "I took three tests earlier today, just to be certain. We're going to have a baby."

Justin leapt to his feet, took her hands, and pulled her into his arms. He dropped kisses on her face and neck, then knelt to kiss her belly. "I'm going to be a father," he said joyously

"You're happy?"

"Sweetheart, you've just made me the happiest man alive."

She hadn't thought he could be any more perfect, but then he went and proved her wrong.

"Congratulations, Daddy," she whispered.

"Congratulations, future Mrs. Simons."

In the dim light cast by the crackling fire, Emily and Justin started the new year the same way they'd started the previous one. Nothing had changed, and yet *everything* had changed. Because they had an eternity together, and two precocious cats and an unborn baby to share it with.

Nothing could beat that.

THE END

ACCIDENTALLY YOURS EXCERPT

Aria wrapped the camera cord around her wrist and strolled onto the Lakeview property, now owned by Lockwood Holdings Limited. It didn't have a driveway yet, and, courtesy of a long, hot summer, the grass was more brown than green. Technically, she wasn't allowed to be here, but, she'd reasoned, it couldn't hurt to pop over for a few minutes to take some photos. Maybe she could superimpose the concept plan of the shopping complex over a photo of the empty lot. Great photography equaled more attention to her article and, hopefully, a promotion. The response to her first article had been crazy. Whether people agreed with it or not, everyone had an opinion.

Flipping her sunglasses over her eyes to shield them from the sun, Aria looked down on Itirangi. Sometimes she wondered if it wouldn't benefit from an upgrade—a few more modern amenities. At the moment, the newer buildings stood out like scars on the landscape, while many of the older buildings were in need of painting, with tussocks in the gardens and scrub that grew unchecked. There was a certain wilderness about Itirangi. Aria thought it was beautiful. And, considering the booming tourist trade, she wasn't alone in her view.

She pondered her next story. She needed to provide the public with more details about the development. She'd done her research and now she was here, searching for inspiration. Wandering around the edge of the property, she snapped photos of the yard, then walked to the highest point and stood on tiptoes. She gazed out toward the lake, over the cottages with overrun lawns and the boutique shops in hundred-year-old buildings. The shimmering lake lapped at the shore. Behind the mass of water, mountains towered brown and green, blending into the horizon. It dazzled her. No wonder someone wanted to build in this spot. They would make a killing.

A sparrow swooped into a tree, and she shot a picture of it mid-flight. Perfect. She was certain one of these photos would be exactly what she needed to liven up her article. While tucking the camera away, she heard a scuffle. Peering over her shoulder, she jumped when she saw a man standing a few yards away. She took a quick step backwards and trod on a stick which rolled under her foot. Her legs gave out beneath her, and she landed on her bottom. *Dammit!* She cursed her clumsiness, a trait it seemed she'd never grow out of. Her butt throbbed. She looked up to introduce herself. And up. And up.

The man loomed over her. He pushed a hand through brown hair tipped with gold, his sky-blue eyes wide in disbelief which slowly turned to disdain as he peered down the length of his perfectly placed nose at her. His full lips pursed, exaggerating a cupid's bow. Five o'clock shadow dusted his cheeks, and his black coat and silk tie were impeccable. The dark colors complimented his golden skin. She couldn't help staring.

Who was he?

No one dressed like this in Itirangi. Even the businessmen wore casual clothes. Jeans and shirts. This man came from another world. A god among mere mortals, gorgeous enough to drive god-fearing women to sin.

～

Elijah wasn't sure whether to be angry at having his peaceful night interrupted or intrigued by the woman at his feet. She had been standing tall at the end of the paddock, like a queen surveying her domain. Except, up close, she was less of a queen and more… Well, odd. Wearing an absurdly fluffy pink jersey with purple leggings, she'd presented her well-formed behind to him as he'd approached unnoticed. Now, she was sitting in the dirt with her hair falling over her face, peering up at him. How bizarre.

He felt a brief flash of sympathy, but it was tempered by annoyance. It had been a long day, and he'd had enough. Not a people-person at the best of times, when he was tired, he preferred to be alone.

Reluctantly, he reached down to help her up. She laid a small, warm hand in his. "Are you okay?" he asked.

"Fine," she replied, her cheeks flushing a delicate shade of pink. "Thanks."

She flicked her long dark hair as she straightened, the curls corkscrewing over her shoulders. Several inches shorter than he, she squinted up into his face, wrinkling her small, upturned nose. Her eyes were brown with flecks of green that flared as she held his gaze. The woman was prettier than he had imagined based on the outlandish outfit.

"What were you doing?" he asked.

"Taking photos." She gestured helplessly at the camera that was still on the ground where she'd fallen. She knelt to pick it up, her leggings tightening over her butt.

"There are better viewpoints of the lake," he told her. This was a nice spot, to be sure. That was why he'd bought it. But there were plenty of nice lookouts much easier to access near the lakefront.

"I know that," she replied indignantly. "I'm a local."

Eli raised an eyebrow. She looked vaguely familiar. "Then, why the camera?"

She glanced away. "I'm doing some research for an article. I work for the paper."

"Look at me."

She started at his sudden command, and her eyes went to his. He jolted in recognition. She was the journalist who'd written that blasphemous article, without a doubt. What the hell was she doing here?

"Did you know this is private land?" he asked, willing to give her the benefit of the doubt this once.

"I know," she admitted with an impish smile. "You won't tell on me, will you?"

He looked up at the sky, jaw clenched. Did she have another awful article in the works? What had he done to deserve this? He tugged on a handful of hair and lowered his gaze back to her. "Tell who, Miss Simons?" he asked. "You've already told on yourself. I'm Elijah Lockwood. This is my property."

"How do you know my name?" she demanded. Then she paled. "*Lockwood*?" She seemed to pull herself together and stuck out a hand. "Nice to meet you. I'm Aria Simons."

"I know," he said impatiently. "You're the journalist who's trying to ruin me."

Her jaw dropped. "I'm not trying to ruin you. I don't know why you'd think that."

"Your bleeding-heart article in yesterday's paper. It wasn't exactly open-minded."

"It wasn't untrue, either," she said, eyeing the exit as if she were considering making a run for it. "I presented one side of the argument. Not the only side."

Eli wanted to rail at her. Could he not get a break? His day had been long enough without adding reporters to the mix.

"You'll print a retraction in tomorrow's paper," he said firmly.

The reporter bristled. Her spine straightened, and her eyes gleamed. "I'm working on a series of articles, Mr. Lockwood, and there's a lot riding on it." He snorted derisively, and her eyes flashed before she continued, "I'll write about every aspect of this development, but I'll do it in my own time, and I'll certainly not print a retraction. I'm not ashamed of my work."

He scowled and crossed his arms. "Suit yourself. There are other ways to fix the problems you've made."

"Look." When she took hold of his arm, her nearness overwhelmed him. His palms started sweating, and he tucked them more firmly into the crooks of his elbows. Did she not understand personal boundaries? "I haven't been trying to make problems for you," she said. "I'm only doing my job. Your development is big news around here. We're a small community, so you shouldn't have expected anything else."

Eli supposed she was right. She had a job to do, and so did he. Clearly, she wasn't going to be as cooperative as he'd hoped. Not that he should have expected anything else. The media hadn't treated him kindly in the past. Never mind. He'd find another way.

Eli's gaze wandered down her body. She was slim but rounded in all the right places, and her body was nicely displayed by the tight, bright clothes. His fingers tingled with the desire to touch her, even as her touch on his arm unsettled him. Though her job offended him, he couldn't deny that her body appealed to him on a visceral level.

"I don't know much about small towns," he drawled. "But I do know business, and I've made this town my business. You'd better get used to having me around."

Aria didn't like men who thought they could get their way simply because they were rich and powerful—and, okay, ridiculously good-looking. They ticked her off. Her fingers curled tighter into his arm.

He spoke again, his voice no more than a rumble. "You know you're still on my property, right?"

Dropping her hand, she reeled backwards. What a beast. She'd only wanted to have a look around and get out of there. It was hardly worth kicking up such a fuss about.

"I'm leaving," she said curtly. "I shouldn't have come. I didn't realize it would upset anyone."

Elijah Lockwood shrugged one perfectly clad shoulder. "I don't like reporters. Especially nosy ones. Trouble always follows them." He pulled a card from his coat pocket and pressed it into her palm. At his touch, jitters shot up her arm. Had a spark passed between them? Static electricity? She flinched away, unwilling to analyze the moment further. "If you have any questions about my development, call this number. Get your information firsthand."

Aria nodded, then brushed past him. Elijah Lockwood, CEO of Lockwood Holdings Limited.

Pity. He was such a good-looking brute.

ACKNOWLEDGMENTS

Thank you to my husband, for putting up with me writing this story during our honeymoon. Thank you for reading the first draft and giving me your unfiltered opinion about what needed work. Thanks to my beta readers for the feedback, support and encouragement. Thanks to Serena W and Kate S for your help with editing and polishing Emily and Justin's story, and for being so constructive. Thanks to my family and friends for their support during the past few years as I've slowly dared to tell people about my books and enter the big, wide world of authoring. Thank you to the wonderful writing community for being so giving, and to the authors and professionals who've helped teach me all I needed to know to get this far.

ABOUT THE AUTHOR

Alexa Rivers writes about genuine characters living messy, imperfect lives and earning hard-won happily ever afters. Most of her books are set in small towns, and she lives in one of these herself. She shares a house with a neurotic dog and a husband who thinks he's hilarious.

When she's not writing, she enjoys traveling, baking, eating too much chocolate, cuddling fluffy animals, drinking excessive amounts of tea, and absorbing herself in fictional worlds.